Stan Barstow was bor
in the West Riding of
married and has a sol
After working in the e
industry, mainly as a
became a full-time writer in 1962.

His first novel, *A Kind of Loving*, was
published in 1960. Since then he has
published three volumes of short
stories and nine more novels, including
*A Raging Calm, Joby, A Brother's Tale,
Just You Wait and See* and *Give Us
This Day*. His work is read and studied
widely in schools. He has been
published in the United States and
translated into nine European
languages. The Open University has
conferred on Stan Barstow an
Honorary Degree of Master of Arts.

He has won The Royal Television
Society Award for Writers on two
occasions and The Writers' Guild and
BAFTA Awards for his television
dramatizations, notably, *Joby, A
Raging Calm* and for Winifred Holtby's
South Riding.

A Kind of Loving became a feature
film (director John Schlesinger) and a
ten-part television serial. *A Brother's
Tale* was also televised in three
episodes.

Author photograph by Neil Barstow.

Also by Stan Barstow

A KIND OF LOVING
THE WATCHERS ON THE SHORE
THE RIGHT TRUE END
THE DESPERADOES
THE GLAD EYE and other stories
JOBY
A RAGING CALM
JUST YOU WAIT AND SEE
A BROTHER'S TALE
GIVE US THIS DAY

and published by Black Swan

A Season With Eros

Stan Barstow

BLACK SWAN

A SEASON WITH EROS

A BLACK SWAN BOOK 0 552 99188 0

Originally published in Great Britain
by Michael Joseph Ltd

PRINTING HISTORY

Michael Joseph edition published 1971
Corgi edition published 1973
Corgi edition reissued 1977
Black Swan edition published 1990

This book is set in 11/12 pt Mallard
by Colset Private Limited, Singapore.

Black Swan Books are published by
Transworld Publishers Ltd., 61–63
Uxbridge Road, Ealing, London W5 5SA, in
Australia by Transworld Publishers
(Australia) Pty. Ltd., 15–23 Helles Avenue,
Moorebank, NSW 2170, and in
New Zealand by Transworld Publishers
(N.Z.) Ltd., Cnr. Moselle and Waipareira
Avenues, Henderson, Auckland.

Printed and bound in Great Britain by
Cox & Wyman Ltd, Reading

Contents

Some of these stories have been broadcast by the BBC. Acknowledgements for those which have been published elsewhere are made to: *Argosy*, *Flair*, the *Guardian*, *Today*, the *Sunday Citizen*, and *Weekend*.

A Season with Eros

Ruffo had waited a long time, kept at bay through his two-year courtship of that girl whose body turned men's heads in the street by the discipline imposed by her cold-eyed watchful mother. A certain amount of boy-girl contact was expected, even approved of: holding hands while watching television in her front room; kisses and tight straining cuddles when the parents were absent; but any attempt to get closer to Maureen than the clutching of her resilient flesh through her clothes was met with an automatic and persistent response: 'No, I can't.' 'Why not?' 'Me mam says I've to wait till I get married.' Beyond this Ruffo found it impossible to go. At best she was stupid, childlike in her reiteration of 'Me mam says . . .'; at worst Ruffo wondered whether in her he had found that most sexually maddening of combinations – a girl whose body yelled promise but whose mind and emotions had no real interest in the subject at all. Exasperated, he drew away from her until his continual casual excuses for not seeing her made his neglect obvious and she, ingenuous in her directness, faced him with it.

'I don't see much point.'

'Oh . . . What's made you change your mind?'

'Your mother. She runs your life for you.'

'She's only trying to do her best for me. Anyway, if that's all you want me for . . .'

'If that's all I want you for I've been seeing you a long time for bugger-all, haven't I?' Ruffo said. 'If you want the truth, I can't stand it any more.'

7

'I've told you, I don't think it's right when you're not married.'

'You mean your mam doesn't.'

'Well, I've always taken notice of what she says.'

'I'm not talking about going the whole hog,' Ruffo said. 'But one thing leads to another, doesn't it?'

Ruffo might have looked at the mother and discerned, more than the person who was keeping him from what he wanted, the woman the daughter could become. But he saw only, behind the canteen buildings where they had met, the creature of his long-repressed desire, the pout of her lips, the rise and fall of her breasts under the thin nylon overall, and he knew that he must have her.

'We'd better get married, then.'

'Oh!' She took it with apparent surprise as though she'd been prepared to go on as they were indefinitely. 'Well, we'd better get engaged first.'

'I don't want any long engagements dragging on. We've been seeing each other for two years now.'

'But we've nowhere to live. And no stuff collected.'

'I'll find somewhere.'

'I suppose me mam 'ud let us live at our house for a while.'

'No,' Ruffo said. 'We want to be on our own. I'll find somewhere.'

He began scanning the property columns of the evening newspaper and asking round among the men in the engineering shop. In the meantime, Maureen broke the news to her mother, who said that Ruffo ought to make his intentions public by buying her a ring. The thirty pounds that this cost Ruffo he parted with grudgingly, feeling that it was money he could ill-afford. Houses were expensive and whatever they found they would need all the cash they could scrape together to put in it even the necessary minimum of furniture. He worked all the overtime offered him, cut out his weekly drinking night with his mates, and stopped taking Maureen anywhere it cost money. He didn't smoke, so there was no saving to be made there. Thinking that he should have a

8

clear idea of their combined resources, he asked Maureen about her savings, only to find to his dismay that was she still giving her wages to her mother, who returned her a weekly sum of pocket money which she spent on make-up and small luxuries.

'Me mam always said I could start paying me own way when I was twenty-one,' Maureen said. 'And, of course, that's still a couple of months off.'

'So you're coming to me empty handed.'

'I've a few sheets an' pillow-cases 'at me mam's giving me.'

'That's bloody generous of her.'

'An' of course they'll be paying for the wedding.'

Ruffo thought with some regret of the passing of the dowry system. 'What we need is brass,' he said. 'Hard cash, to pay the deposit on a house and furnish it.'

'They're building some lovely ones up Lime Lane,' she said.

'You must be out of your mind. They're a four-and-a-half thousand quid touch. That means at least five hundred deposit.'

Which Ruffo hadn't got. And as he went on looking and making enquiries he came to see the nature of the trap he had laid for himself. Marriage to Maureen had seemed an obvious way of getting what he wanted; but marriage was not, it seemed, a state easily achieved. And now he was worse off than before: still deprived, but robbed by that engagement ring of the freedom to come and go which he had held in reserve and thought of as a bargaining counter.

Then he struck lucky, hearing from a workmate about a house occupied by an old lady who had just been taken into hospital with what looked like a fatal illness.

'You want to get round there. Put your word in afore anybody else does.'

'I'll bet there's five hundred after it already.'

'You never know. You'll lose nowt by trying.'

And gain nothing if I don't, Ruffo thought.

He went straight to the owner, a wholesale grocer

who received him in the hall of his grand new bungalow.

'A house? I don't know that there's one coming vacant.'

Ruffo saw the delicacy of the situation and chose his words accordingly. 'An old lady lived there. I heard she'd died in hospital.'

'It's news to me if she's dead.' The man eyed him shrewdly. 'You mean you want to be first in line if she does pop off? By God, you're quick off the mark, some of you. You don't let the breath leave the corpse.'

'I expect there's plenty before me, anyway,' Ruffo said. 'You don't stand much chance of dropping across a house to rent nowadays.'

'Why don't you buy one?'

'Because I haven't got the money. If I could find a place in the meantime it'd give me a chance to save up. Everybody's got to start somewhere.'

'Otherwise it's in-laws, is that it?'

Ruffo shook his head. 'I'm not having that.'

'No, happen you're wise there. What did you say your name was?'

'Billy Roughsedge.'

'Did they call your father Walter?'

'Aye, that's right.'

'I knew him. Played bowls with him many a time in days gone by. Dead now, though, isn't he?'

'Aye, me mother as well. I live with me married sister.'

'Well, like I say, I don't know that there's anything coming vacant, but I'll keep you in mind. Give us your address.'

Ruffo thought little more of it; but a fortnight later he got a note through the post to say that the house was now empty and if he still wanted it would he go to see the agents.

It stood in a terrace on a back street; two rooms down, two up; no hot water, and a lavatory – shared with another family – in the long communal yard. Everything in that area was probably due for demolition during the next few years, Ruffo thought. But programmes like that had a way of being put back and before then he and Maureen would have got out; or if they hadn't the Corporation would be compelled to offer them alternative accommodation, along with everyone else. It was a start, a place to live, on their own; nothing to shout about but no worse than either of them had known before at some time in their lives. And it could be made cosy enough.

They fixed a date for the wedding and Ruffo went through the house stripping paint and wallpaper and redecorating from top to bottom. Before that, with the help of a friend, he pulled out the black old range and replaced it with a tiled fireplace. He also fitted over the corner sink an electric water-heater which he'd bought second-hand through the small ads in the evening paper. For their furniture they went to sale rooms. Maureen would have liked more new pieces, but Ruffo showed her the balance in his Post Office Bank book and made it clear that he did not intend to start out with a load of hire-purchase debts.

Marriage suited Ruffo. He had lived for too long in someone else's house; and though the people involved were his sister and his brother-in-law there had been occasional small points of friction. Their children were growing up, needing more space, and he'd had for some time the feeling that he was beginning to get in the way. Now he had his own place and a wife: a home where he could do as he liked, and as much sex as he wanted with the girl he'd always wanted it with. Any lingering fears that she might not find pleasure in it were quickly dispelled. With the wedding over, and a ring on her finger, she became willing and compliant, following wherever he led with no more protest than an occasional indulgent 'Ruffo! Whatever will you think of next?'

For Ruffo, in possession of her at last, had thrown himself from the cliff of frustrated deprivation into a protracted sexual binge. Impossible for him to have too much of her, he liked her to go without pants and bra in

11

the house so that at any moment he could catch at her, one hand into her blouse to knead at a breast, the other under her skirt where, to her coy whinnies of delight, his probing fingers would draw the juices of her instant response. His fondling of her like this in the early evening, sometimes by the sink as she washed-up after their meal, would often lead to his taking her there and then, she standing, back arched, legs apart and braced, panting to the electric contact of his flesh. On other evenings, with the fire built high and the television picture flickering silently in the corner, she would dress for him in items of exotic underwear and lingerie which he bought through the post to accentuate or semi-conceal the objects of his never-ending desire: briefs whose flimsy transparency held like a dark stain the tufty triangle of her crotch; brassieres cut low to lift those already splendidly jutting breasts and thrust them up and out, rampant-nippled, like great pale tropical fruits. Nor did any of this tire them for later when, in bed together, his earlier spending gave him a restraint which could carry them through an hour of intertwined limbs, bringing her time after time until it seemed to her that each night was one long moan of love.

He was confident, in command; his ego strutted and he carried himself with an assurance which bordered on the insolent. It was not lost on other women: Ruffo felt their awareness. One who served behind the counter of the canteen watched him as he stood in line for his meal. When he got to the head of the queue she put a double portion of cabbage on his plate.

'There y'are. That'll put some lead in your pencil.'

'I've got plenty, thanks.'

'You could run short, the way you're going on.'

Ruffo's head came up. 'What d'you mean by that?'

'Nay, lad, I'm only kidding you. If you've any to spare you can bring it round to my house. My old man's forgotten what it's all about.'

Ruffo grinned. 'Sorry. It's all spoken for.'

'Aye, well,' the woman said with mock regret, 'you can but try.'

Ruffo challenged Maureen that evening.

'What have you been saying to them women in the canteen?'

'Oh, you know how they kid about things like that, Ruffo. They got on at me and somehow or other it came out that we do it every day. Sometimes more. They're only jealous.'

'Aye,' Ruffo said, his hands on her. 'I look after you well, don't I?'

'Mmm, you do. It's lovely.'

'It's better than that,' Ruffo said. 'It's bloody perfect.'

He was happy. He worked hard, saving all the money he could; but beyond this he did not worry about the future. Today was what mattered. Yesterday was gone; tomorrow would come when it came. They were both young; there was plenty of time for everything. He lived for the present; for each evening when, secure and warm in their own home, they could indulge in their sexual games. Maureen was his now; he moulded her to his desire, was masterful in the way he took her. She seemed to want it that way, content in being the focus of most of his waking thoughts. A knowing little half-smile would often appear momentarily in her eyes when he touched her, as though she knew very well the power her compliance gave her over him.

One evening they were lying together on the hearthrug when Maureen's mother came unexpectedly to the door. Ruffo grabbed his clothes and went upstairs while Maureen put on her dressing-gown and let her in.

'I was just getting washed and changed,' Maureen explained.

Her mother glanced round the room, her nostrils dilating, as though she could smell their passion in the air. Ruffo, coming down the stairs a few moments later, heard a part of their conversation.

'He's not, er, asking too much of you, is he?'

'What do you mean?'

'Well, some men, you know, they're greedy. They never leave a woman alone.'

'Oh, I see! No, it's not like that at all.'

13

'As long as you're all right. There are other things in life, you know.'

Tell her you love it, Ruffo thought. Tell her to mind her own business. He opened the door and walked into the room.

It was a few evenings later that Maureen said, 'Ruffo, I think we ought to save it till we're in bed.'

'Eh?'

'Well, you know the other night, when me mam came; I didn't know where to put meself for a minute or two. Suppose we'd forgotten to slip the latch and she'd walked straight in?'

'Oh, now . . .'

'I mean, she knew what we were doing, Ruffo. I know she knew.'

'Well, what about it? Come o-on . . .'

He got his way, but for the first time he felt in her submission an unspoken reproach. There was little response: she was acquiescent, no more, and he was alone, with her as the passive instrument of his pleasure.

He had no time to resolve this before she went down with a heavy cold which turned into influenza and confined her to bed for a week. Her mother came every day to tidy the house, do their washing, and attend to Maureen while Ruffo was out at work. Then there came an evening when she was fully recovered and Ruffo thought it was time he broke his sexual fast. He went upstairs to look in her lingerie drawer and came back down again to ask her:

'Where's your black sling bra?'

'Which one do you mean?'

'You know which I mean. The one I sent away for.'

'Oh, that one.' She wasn't looking at him. 'Ruffo, me mam found it when she was sorting out the washing.'

'Oh, did she?'

'She said she didn't know how I could wear a thing like that. She said it was the sort of thing a prostitute wears.'

'How does she know what a prostitute wears? And what's it got to do with her, anyway?'

'Nothing, I suppose. But still . . .'

'And where is it, then?'

'I . . . I burned it. I put it on the fire the other day.'

He was incredulous. 'You did what? What the hell made you do that?'

'I wanted to be rid of it, I just didn't fancy wearing it any more.'

'Nobody was asking you to go out in it. It was for me.'

'I know. All the same . . .'

Ruffo went back upstairs and had another look in the drawer.

'You've made a clean sweep, haven't you?'

Still she couldn't meet his eyes. 'I . . . I felt . . . well, sort of dirty.'

'Oh, you did!' Ruffo said, irate now. 'Did I make you feel mucky when I bought 'em for you and you put 'em on for me?'

'Well, no, not then.'

'But you would now?'

'It was all right, Ruffo. I knew you liked it. But we can still make love without that sort of thing.'

'You'll be bloody getting undressed in the dark next,' Ruffo said, the anger bursting out of him.

'There's no need to exaggerate.'

'Look,' Ruffo said, 'haven't we had a good time since we got married? You and me. Haven't we had a good time?'

'Of course we have.'

'Well, why let somebody else stick their nose in?'

'It's not that . . .'

'Well, what is it, then?'

'Give up, Ruffo. Stop getting on at me. I've got a headache.'

Ruffo carried his anger to bed with him. For the first time they lay back to back, not touching.

He was surly and uncommunicative during the next few days, speaking only when necessary. He ate his

15

evening meal in silence then looked at television for three or four hours before going early to bed. One night he went down to the local pub, something he'd done only a couple of times since they were married, and came back uncertain in his movements. Maureen began to stay in bed another half an hour in the mornings, leaving him to get himself off to work. It was less retaliation on her part than a wish not to provoke him, to let him work off his mood in his own time. For she had something to tell him and when the weekend arrived without any change she forced herself to speak.

'Ruffo, I know you're out of sorts with me, and I'm sorry. But there's something you'll have to know. I think I'm pregnant.'

'Well, that's bloody marvellous,' Ruffo said.

'Is that all you've got to say?'

'I thought we were going to wait till we'd moved to a decent house and settled down a bit.'

'I know, but—'

'We're only . . . we're only kids ourselves! What do we want a baby yet for?'

'That's all very well. But if I'm having one, I am. You can't always plan these things, can you?'

' 'Course you can,' Ruffo said. 'Ninety-nine times out of a—' He stopped and, for the first time in days, looked directly at her. 'You didn't do it on purpose, did you?'

'What makes you think—?'

'You did,' Ruffo said. 'You bloody did. I can see it written all over your face.'

'Look, Ruffo,' she said eagerly, 'the younger you are when you have your family the more time you have together when they've grown up and you're on your own again.'

It was like a doctrine she had learned. He stared at her, aghast. 'Who cares about what happens then? We might all be bloody dead by then. I want my time now, while I'm young.'

'You don't want a family at all, do you?'

'In a year or two,' Ruffo said, 'when we're better

placed and we've enjoyed being together, just the two of us.'

'But we've had that, haven't we?'

'Aye, we have,' Ruffo said. 'We've had it, all right.'

It was all going, vanishing before his eyes. He looked at Maureen as though he'd never really seen her before. He had thought he was moulding her but now, in a flash of intuition, he perceived his fate as a function of the phases of her life. He was too young for a glass case marked 'husband'.

He brooded on it for a couple of days; then one morning he turned over in bed when the alarm clock rang and said he wasn't feeling well. When Maureen had gone out to work he got up, shaved and dressed, packed his personal belongings in a case, wrote a note for her, and left.

The note said that he would not be coming back, but that when he had settled down elsewhere he would write again and arrange to pay maintenance for the child. Maureen's mother wanted her to put the police on his trail so that she could sue for maintenance for herself, but Maureen refused to do this. She had her job and she gave up the house and sold its contents and moved back in with her parents. Six months later she heard from Ruffo who was now in Australia, working on a hydroelectric power scheme. He said he would be willing if she wanted to divorce him, since she was still very young and would no doubt want to marry again. There were times when she felt a vague yearning for Ruffo's loving, but she came to accept that as a stage of her life which had passed; that, and the earlier one of the young unmarried girl single-mindedly keeping herself untouched for her future husband. With the child big in her now she was absorbed in her new role of mother-to-be. And to this she added the unexpected one of deserted wife without too much apparent strain.

17

Twenty Pieces of Silver

When the Misses Norris, in pursuance of their good works, called on little Mrs Fosdyke at her tiny terrace house in Parker Street she answered their discreet knock dressed for going out. They apologized then in their quiet, genteel way and said they would call again. But Mrs Fosdyke beckoned them into the house. 'I've just come in,' she said. 'A minute or two earlier and you'd have followed me down the street.' It was then that the Misses Norris realized that Mrs Fosdyke was dressed in black, the hat shop-bought but the coat probably run up on her own machine, and, as if reading their minds, she said, 'I've just been to a funeral,' and the Misses Norris murmured 'Oh?' for no-one of their acquaintance had died during the past week.

They sat down when asked to, the elder Miss Norris on the edge of the armchair by the table, legs tucked neatly away behind her skirt; the younger Miss Norris upright on a chair by the window. Mrs Fosdyke slipped off her coat and occupied herself with kettle and teapot at the sink in the corner.

'You'll have a cup o'tea?' she asked, the spoon with the second measure poised over the pot.

'Well . . .' the younger Miss Norris began, and her sister said, with the poise and grace of her extra years, 'You're very kind.'

'I hate funerals,' Mrs Fosdyke said conversationally as she poured boiling water into the pot. 'If it's anybody you thought anything of they upset you; and if it's somebody you didn't like you feel a hypocrite.'

She took two more cups and saucers from the cupboard over the sink, wiping them thoroughly on the tea towel before setting them out alongside her own on the oilcloth-covered top of the clothes-wringer under the window.

'Was it a relative?' the younger Miss Norris ventured.

Mrs Fosdyke shook her head. 'No, a friend. A good friend. Mrs Marsden from up Hilltop. Don't know if you knew her. A widow, like me. Her husband died five or six years back. He used to be something in textiles over Bradford way. Quite well-to-do, they were. Poor dear . . . She had cancer, y'know. It was a happy release for her.'

She poured the tea, handing the Misses Norris a cup each and passing the sugar bowl and milk jug to each in turn. She herself remained standing, between the wringer and the sink, the late-morning sun lighting her grey hair below the little black hat.

'Funny,' she said reflectively, between sips. 'Fifteen years I'd known Mrs Marsden and it might only have been a month or two. Funny how friendships start . . .

'I answered an advertisement in the *Argus*, y'know. That's how I came to go in the first place. Jim was alive then and he'd just taken to his wheelchair. I was looking for work but I couldn't take on a full-time job because of having him to see to. So I got a few cleaning jobs that kept me busy six mornings a week. Mrs Marsden's was one of them. Three mornings, I went to her.

'I didn't think I was going to stick it at first. There was nothing wrong with the job or the money, mind; but they hadn't started running buses up to Hilltop at that time, and it was a mile and a half uphill from town. A rare drag, it was, and it seemed to get longer and steeper and harder every morning I went there. Anyway, I needed the money, and that was that.

'I knew when Jim first went down it wouldn't be easy, but I told meself we'd manage. Just so long as I could keep going.'

The Misses Norris, neither of whom had ever done anything more strenuous about a house than vacuum a carpet, murmured in sympathy and understanding and sipped their tea.

'Well, it wasn't too bad when I'd got used to it – the going out and cleaning, I mean. We managed. Mrs Reed next door kept her eye on Jim in the mornings, and I did my own cleaning and my shopping in the afternoons. We'd always been ones for simple pleasures. We liked the chapel. There were the services on Sundays and the Women's Bright Hour on Wednesday afternoons, and I used to park Jim's chair in the porch where he could hear the singing and watch what was going on in the street. And then there were the Saturday-night concerts in the schoolroom – though they don't have so many of them nowadays – and anybody who was willing did a turn. I can see Jim's face now, all flushed and cheerful, his head nodding to the music . . .'

'He was a brave and cheerful man, Mrs Fosdyke,' said the elder Miss Norris. 'We all admired his courage.'

'Aye, aye. Well, of course, you know all about the chapel and the Bright Hour, an' that.

'Well, Mrs Marsden made me realize you could be well off and still unhappy. That you could be lacking in peace and quietness of mind even with no money worries, and a husband in good health.

'I remember the first time we talked as woman to woman. It came up because it was a Wednesday and I wanted to finish prompt on twelve so's I could get done at home in time for the Bright Hour. It was my first week with Mrs Marsden and I had to explain the position.

' "I don't mind stopping a bit extra on Mondays and Fridays, if you need me," I said, "but I shouldn't like to miss my Bright Hour on a Wednesday."

' "I'm sure I shouldn't like to be the one to keep you away," she said, and there was something a bit odd in her voice that puzzled me. But nothing more was said till the Wednesday after, and then she brought it up herself, and this queer something in her voice was there again, and I asked her if she didn't go to a place of worship herself, then.

20

' "I used to," she said, "a long time ago. I was brought up in the Church. I was on several committees. I worked like a slave for it."

' "And whatever made you give it up, then?" I said.

' "I lost all reason for going," she said.

'I was a bit shocked then. "You mean," I said, "you lost your faith in God?"

'As soon as I'd said it, of course, I was sorry I'd pried. It was none of my business, after all.

'And then, after a minute, she said "Yes." Just like that: straight out.

'I remember clearly as if it were yesterday, knocking off the vacuum-cleaner and looking at her. I knew lots of people who never went to either chapel or church, but I'd never come face to face with one who said straight out she was atheist. Because, that's what it amounted to.

'So I said to her, "Well, I mean, it's none of my business, but what ever did that to you?"

'And she rolled her duster up and her face went all hard. "I had a boy," she said. "He died."

'I could feel for her. "That's terrible," I said. "But lots of people—"

' "But this was *my* boy," she said. "For ten years we prayed for a child. We prayed and prayed, and then eventually he came. He was an imbecile. He died when he was three. Have you ever had an idiot child, Mrs Fosdyke?" she said, and she was so twisted up with bitterness inside her I could hardly bear to look at her.

'So I said, no, I hadn't. "But I've seen a fine God-fearing man struck down in his prime and condemned to spend the rest of his days in a wheelchair," I said. "I can sympathize with you, Mrs Marsden."

' "And yet you still believe," she said, and she was full of impatience and anger. "How can you believe in a God of love who allows these things?"

' "Wouldn't it be easy to believe if everything in the world was fine and grand?" I said. "Anybody could believe with no trouble at all. But that's not God's way. He has to send suffering to try us, to steel us and purify us."

21

' "Oh, stuff and nonsense," she said. "I've heard it all before. What does a little child know of these things?"

' "I know, I know," I said. "It's hard to understand. But how can he make an exception for children? There has to be danger for them, just like grown-ups."

'So she just turned her back on me then and polished away at the dresser. And then she spun round on me in a second. "But how can you reconcile yourself to it?" she said. "How can you accept it?"

' "It's one of those things you can't argue out, Mrs Marsden,"I said. "You can talk about it till Domesday and get no forrader. It's something you've got to feel. And I reckon you either feel it or you don't. How can I accept it, you say. Why, what else can I do? If I lose that, I've nothing else left." And I looked at her and I said, "But you do miss it, don't you, you poor dear?"

'I'd gone a bit too far there. She drew herself up and went all chilly. She was a very thin woman, you know, and she could look very proud when she set herself. "I don't need your pity, thank you," she said. "What you believe is your own business . . . You can finish the carpet now," she said, "if you don't mind."

'I was sorry afterwards that it had happened. I was beginning to find in this business of going into other women's homes that a friendly but respectful relationship was the best on both sides, and I didn't want to spoil anything . . .

'Another cup? Oh, go on; it'll just be wasted if you don't . . . That's right.'

The two Misses Norris allowed their cups to be refilled, and since they had nothing else to do that morning which could not be done later, settled back in comfort to hear whatever else Mrs Fosdyke would tell them of her relationship with the late Mrs Marsden.

'She wouldn't leave it alone, though,' Mrs Fosdyke said. 'She seemed to be waiting for chances to bring it up again. She seemed to have to let out that sourness and bitterness inside her. I didn't like it, and I did think of leaving her. But I decided I could stand it. She wasn't a bad employer, and I needed the money. Pride has to take a bit of a back seat when you're in a position I was in then.

'Anyway, I'd been working for her for six months, and one Wednesday I went up there as usual. The mornings passed quickly, and it seemed like twelve o'clock came almost before I'd gotten started. As I was putting my things on to go, Mrs Marsden remembered two things at once. She wanted me to leave one of her husband's suits at the cleaners, and she had to nip out to see a neighbour who'd be going out at any minute.

'So she came into the kitchen with the suit draped all any-old-how over her arm. "Here we are," she said. "He hasn't worn it for some time. I'd like to see if it will clean up decently. Now if I don't hurry I shall miss Mrs Wilson. You'll find paper and string in that cupboard; and you might just go through the pockets before you wrap it up. I haven't time, myself." And with a last reminder to drop the latch as I went out, she was off.

'I had a look at the suit then. It looked nearly new to me, and I thought to myself. "Fancy being able to cast aside a suit like this." I hadn't got to the stage of begging clothes, but I was tempted at times. Jim had never had a suit like that in his life.

'Well, I took each part of it in turn and brushed it down with the flat of my hand and went through all the pockets. When I got to the waistcoat I more felt than heard something crackle in one of the pockets, and when I put my fingers in I pulled out a pound note, folded in two. So from thinking about Mr Marsden discarding good clothes I got to thinking about a "carry on" that could allow a pound note to be lost without being missed.

'I popped it down on a corner of the kitchen cabinet and wrapped the suit in brown paper. I found myself glancing sideways at the note. Who knew about it but me? A pound . . . twenty shillings. What was a pound to the Marsdens? And what was a pound to Jim and me? There were few enough ever came our way, and every

23

one was hard earned, every shilling to be held on to till I couldn't help spending it. Things had been tighter than usual lately, as well. We'd had a lot of expense. I took the note into my hand and thought of all it could buy. Fruit for Jim, and a bit of tobacco – always a special treat. And he needed new underclothes. And I'd planned to get him a bottle of the tonic wine that seemed to buck him up so.

'So, I stood there in Mrs Marsden's kitchen with her husband's pound note screwed up in a little ball in my hand where nobody else could see it; and it was just as though there was nothing else in the world but that note and my need of it.'

Mrs Fosdyke's voice had grown softer and now it died away altogether as she stopped speaking and gazed out through the window. The two sisters exchanged a swift glance before she stirred and turned to put her empty cup on the draining-board.

'Well, that was a Wednesday, like I said. And on the Friday I went up to the house again. I was there at nine, my usual time. I remember distinctly that it was a rainy morning. Not heavy rain, but that thin, fine stuff that seems to wet you through more thoroughly than an out-and-out downpour. Anyway, I was soaked by the time I got there, and when I'd changed into my working-shoes, I took my coat upstairs to let it drip into the bath. Then I helped Mrs Marsden with the few breakfast pots and we got going on the downstairs rooms, like we always did on a Friday.

'She was a bit quiet that morning, Mrs Marsden was, and I thought perhaps she wasn't feeling too well. At eleven we knocked off for five minutes and went into the kitchen for a cup of tea and a biscuit. And then Mrs Marsden said, just casual like, "By the way," she said, "Mr Marsden seems to think he left some money in that suit you took to the cleaners. Did you find anything when you looked through the pockets?"

'I'd clean forgotten about it till she mentioned it. I put my cup down and got up and felt under one of the canisters on the shelf. "You didn't see it, then?" I said. "I popped it up there on Wednesday. I meant to mention it, but I get more forgetful every day. That's all there was: just the odd note." I wondered she didn't notice the tremble in my fingers as I handed it to her.

'She spread the note out by her plate and said she'd give it to Mr Marsden when he came home. And I said it was funny that he'd bethought himself about it after all that time. I remembered she'd said he hadn't worn the suit for some while.

' "Well," she said, "you see -er-er . . ." And she got all sort of tongue-tied, and then I knew there was something wrong somewhere. I didn't like the look on her face, for a start. And then it came over me, all at once.

' "Why," I said, "I believe you put that money in your husband's suit. I don't think he knows anything about it. You put it there deliberately, hoping I'd take it and say nothing."

'She went red then; her face coloured like fire. "I have to test the honesty of my servants," she said, sort of proud like, but uneasy under it.

'And it got my rag out, that did. I was blazing mad. "Well you tested mine," I said. "And if it's any joy to you, I'll admit I was sorely tempted. Isn't it enough that you should lose your way without making me lose mine? A pound, Mrs Marsden," I said. "Twenty pieces of silver. Is that my price, d'you think? They gave Judas thirty!"

'She got up. "I don't have to take this kind of talk from you," she said, and brushed past me and ran upstairs.

'I sat down at the table and put my head in my hands. I was near to tears. I couldn't understand it. I just couldn't understand what had made her do it. And I said a little prayer of thanks. "O God," I said, "only You knew how near I was."

'In a few minutes I got up and went and listened at the foot of the stairs. I went up to the bathroom and got my coat. I stood for a minute then. There was no place for me here in the future. I felt like leaving straight away:

25

walking out without another word. But I was due to a week's wages and I couldn't afford pride of that sort.

'So I called out softly, "Mrs Marsden."

'But there was no reply. I went across the landing to her bedroom door and listened. I could hear something then, but I wasn't quite sure what it was. I called again, and when nobody answered I tapped on the door and went in. She was lying on one of the twin beds with her face to the window. I could tell now it was sobbing I'd heard and her shoulders shook as I stood and watched her. There was something about her that touched me right to the quick, and I put my coat down and went to her and put my hand on her shoulder. "There, there," I said, "don't take on so. There's no harm done." I sat down behind her on the bed, and all at once she put her hand up and took mine. "Don't go away," she said. "Don't leave me now."

'I remember just the feeling I had then. It was like a great rush of joy: the sort of feeling you get when you know you're wanted, that somebody needs you.

' "Of course I won't leave you," I said, "Of course I won't." '

Mrs Fosdyke sighed and turned from the window. 'And I never did,' she said. 'I never did.'

She looked at each of the sisters in turn. 'Well,' she said, a bashful little smile coming to her lips. 'I've never told anybody about that before. But this morning sort of brought it all back. And she's gone beyond harm now, poor dear.'

She glanced at the clock on the mantelpiece. 'Gracious, look at the time! And me keeping you sat with my chatter.'

'But what a lovely story,' said the younger Miss Norris, who was of a romantic turn of mind. 'It's like something out of the Bible.'

'Well, that's as maybe,' Mrs Fosdyke said briskly, 'but I'm sure you didn't call to hear me tell the tale.'

'As a matter of fact,' the elder Miss Norris said, drawing a sheaf of papers from her large handbag, 'we're organizing the collection for the orphanage and we wondered if you could manage this district again this year. We know how busy you are.'

'Well' – Mrs Fosdyke put her finger to her chin – 'I suppose I *could* fit it in.'

'You're such a *good* collector, Mrs Fosdyke,' the younger Miss Norris said. 'Everyone gives so generously when you go round.'

'Aye, well, I suppose I can manage it,' Mrs Fosdyke said, and the Misses Norris beamed at her.

'Oh, we know the willing hearts and hands, Mrs Fosdyke,' the elder sister said.

'I suppose you do,' said Mrs Fosdyke, with a hint of dryness in her voice.

'There'll be a place in heaven for you, Mrs Fosdyke,' gushed the younger Miss Norris.

'Oh, go on with you.' Mrs Fosdyke said. 'Somebody's got to look out for the poor lambs, haven't they?'

Principle

Mrs Stringer had a hot meal ready for the table at twenty-five past five when the click of the gate told her of her husband Luther's approach. His bad tempered imprecation on the dog, which was lying on the doorstep in the evening sun, told her also what frame of mind he was in.

With the oven-cloth protecting her hands she picked up the stewpot and carried it through into the living-room. 'Your father's in one of his moods, Bessie,' she said to her daughter, who had arrived home a few minutes before and was laying the table for the meal. 'For goodness' sake don't get his back up tonight. I've had a splittin' head all day.'

There was the sound of running water as Luther washed his hands under the kitchen tap, and in a few minutes the three of them were sitting together round the table. Luther had not spoken a word since his entrance and he did not break his silence now until Bessie inadvertently went almost to the heart of the trouble when she said casually:

'Did Bob say anything about coming round tonight?'

Luther was a thickset man of a little above medium height. He had a rather magnificent mane of iron-grey hair which in his youth had been a reddish-blond colour and of which he was still proud. It topped a lean and rather lugubrious face with blue eyes and a thin-lipped mouth which had a tendency to slip easily into disapproval. He loved to argue, for he had opinions on all the topics of the day. But he was also a man who never saw a joke and this, with his baleful, ponderous way of making a point, made him, unconsciously, a source of amusement to the younger of his workmates, among whom he was known as 'Old Misery'.

He chewed in silence now and swallowed before attempting to answer Bessie's questions. Then he said briefly, 'No, he didn't.'

'Didn't he mention it at all?' Bessie asked.

'I haven't spoken to him all day,' Luther said, and blew hard on a forkful of steaming suet dumpling.

'Well, that's funny,' Bessie said, 'an' him working right next to you. Is there summat up, or what?'

'You might say that.' Luther took a mouthful of water. 'They've sent him to Coventry.'

'They've what?' Bessie said, and her mother, taking a sudden interest in the exchange, said, 'But that's miles away. Will he be home weekends?'

'What d'you mean they've sent him to Coventry?' Bessie said.

'Just what I say.'

'But whatever for?'

Luther put his elbow on the table and looked grimly along his fork at Bessie. 'I didn't work yesterday, did I?'

'No, you didn't. But—'

'I didn't work,' Luther said, 'because we had a one-day token strike in support o' t'union wage claim. I didn't work an' none o' t'other union members worked – bar Bob. He went in as usual.'

'And you mean none of you's talking to him just because of that?'

'Aye,' Luther said with heavy sarcasm. 'Just because of that.'

Bessie drew herself up indignantly. 'Well, it's down-right childish, that's what it is. Nobody talking to him because he worked yesterday.'

Luther put down his knife and fork.

'Look here. What do you do wi' a lass when you've no room for her?'

'Well, I . . .'

'Come on,' Luther said. 'Be honest about it.'

'Well, I don't have owt to do with her. But—'

'That's right,' Luther said, picking up his knife and fork and resuming eating now that the point was made for him. 'An' when a lot o' men feels that way about one chap it's called sendin' him to Coventry.'

'You don't mean to say you've fallen in with it, Luther?' Mrs Stringer said.

'I have that,' Luther said, shaking his head in a slow gesture of determination. 'I'm wi' t'men.'

'But Bob's my fiancy,' Bessie wailed.

'Aye, an' my future son-in-law, I'm sorry to say.'

'I must say it does seem a shame 'at you should treat your own daughter's fiancy like that,' said Mrs Stringer, and Luther gave her a look of resigned scorn.

'Now look,' he said, preparing to lay down the law, 'Bob's a member o' t'union. When t'union negotiates a rise in wages Bob gets it. When it gets us an' improvement in conditions, Bob gets them an' all. But when t'union strikes for more brass – not just at Whittakers, not just in Cressley, but all over t'country – Bob goes to work as usual. Now I don't like a chap what does a thing like that. An' when I don't like a chap I have no truck with him.'

'I'll bet nobody give him a chance to put his side of it,' Bessie cried.

'He has no side. There's only one side to this for a union member. He should ha' struck wi' t'rest on us.'

'Well, that's a proper mess,' Bessie muttered. But her mind was now on the more immediate problem. 'I don't know whether I've to go and meet him, or if he's coming here ...'

'I shouldn't think he'll have t'cheek to show his face in here tonight,' Luther said.

But half an hour later, when the table was cleared and Luther had his feet up with his pipe and the evening paper, and Bessie, now made-up for the evening, was still dithering in distress and confusion, there came a knock on the back door and Bob's voice was heard in the kitchen.

Bessie ran out to meet him and Luther raised his paper so that his face was hidden. To his surprise, Bob came right into the living-room as Bessie told him in great detail of her uncertainty about the evening's plans.

'Your dad's told you, then,' Bob said.

'Oh, aye,' Bessie said, 'an' I told him how childish I thought it was. Like a pack o' schoolkids, they all are.'

'A flock o' sheep, more like,' Bob muttered. 'All fallin' in together.'

This brought Luther's paper down to reveal his flashing eyes. 'Aye, all together. How else do you think a union can work?'

'Oh! You'll talk to him now, then?' Bessie said.

'I'm askin' him a question,' Luther said. 'How else does he think a union can work?'

'I don't know an' I don't care,' Bob said. 'I'm fed up o' t'union an' everybody in it.'

'That's a lot o' men, an' there's a fair number on 'em fed up wi' thee, lad. Anyway, happen tha'll not be bothered wi' it for much longer.'

'How d'ye mean?'

'I mean they'll probably call for thi card afore long.'

'Well, good riddance. I never wanted to join in the first place.'

'Why did you, then?'

'Because I couldn't have t'job unless I did. I was forced into it.'

'An' for why?' Luther said. 'Because we don't want a lot o' scroungers an' wasters gettin' t'benefits while we pay t'subscriptions.'

'Who's callin' me a scrounger?' Bob said, with a first show of heat. 'Don't I do as good a day's work as t'next man – an' better?'

'Well, tha can work,' Luther admitted. 'But tha hasn't common sense tha wa' born wi'.'

'Sense! I've enough sense to think for meself an' make up me own mind when there isn't an independent man among t'rest of you.'

'That's what I mean,' Luther said blithely. 'All this talk about independence an' making up your own mind. They like it, y'know. It's playin' right into their hands.'

'Whose hands?'

'T'bosses' hands, I mean. They like chaps 'at's independent; fellers 'at don't agree wi' nobody. They can get 'em on their own an' they haven't as much bargaining power as a rabbit wi' a ferret on its tail.'

'Ah, you're fifty year out o' date,' Bob said impatiently. 'Look, here we are with the cost o' livin' goin' up an' up. We've got to stop somewhere. It's up to somebody to call a halt. But what does t'union do but put in for another wage increase. What we want is restraint.'

'Like there is on profits an' dividends, you mean?'

'What do you know about profits an' dividends?'

'That's it!' Luther cried. 'What *do* I know? What do you know? Nowt. We don't see hardly any of it where we are. We have to take t'word of somebody 'at knows, somebody 'at's paid to study these things. T'union leaders, lad, t'union leaders. An' when they say "Look here, lads, these fellers are coalin' in their profits an' dividends and t'cost o' livin's goin' up an' up an' it's time we had a rise," then we listen to 'em. An' when they say "Strike, lads," we strike. At least, some of us does,' he added with a scornful look at Bob.

'Look,' Bob said, 'I believe in a fair day's work for a fair day's pay.'

'No more na me.'

'An' if t'boss is satisfied with me work he gives me fair pay.'

'He does if t'union's made him.'

'He does without that, if he's a fair man. Look at Mr Whittaker.'

'Aye, let's look,' Luther said. 'I've worked for Whittakers now for thirty years. I know Matthew Whittaker and I knew old Dawson afore him. Neither of 'em's ever had cause to grumble about my work an' by an' large I've had no cause to grumble about them. When t'union's put in a wage claim they've chuntered a bit an' then given us it. But they wouldn't if we hadn't been in force, all thinkin' an' actin' together. There's fair bosses an' there's t'other sort – that I'll grant you. But then again, there's bosses an' there's men. Men think about their wages an bosses think about their profits. It's business, lad. It's life! I'm not blamin' 'em. But you've got to face it: they're on one side an' we're on t'other. An' when we want summat we've got to show 'em we're all together an' we mean to have it. That's what made us all so mad at thee. Everybody out but thee. We listened to t'union an' tha listened to t'bosses callin' for wage restraint.'

'I don't listen to t'bosses,' Bob said. 'I listen to the telly an' read the papers an' make up me own mind.'

'Well, tha reads t'wrong papers, then,' Luther said. 'Tha'll be tellin' me next tha votes Conservative.'

'I don't. I vote Liberal.'

Luther stared at him, aghast. 'Liberal! Good sainted aunts protect us! An' is this t'chap you're goin' to wed?' he said to Bessie.

'As far as I know,' Bessie said, putting her chin up.

'Well, he'll be a fiancy wi'out a job afore long.'

'Why? He worked, didn't he? It's you lot they should sack, not Bob.'

'But you see,' Luther said with enforced patience, 'they can't sack us because there's too many of us. We've a hundred per cent shop up at Whittakers an' t'men'll not work wi' a chap 'at isn't in t'union. An' your Bob won't be in t'union for much longer, or I'm a Dutchman.'

'Well, if that isn't the limit!' Bessie gasped.

'I do think it's a cryin' shame 'at a young chap should be victimized because of his principles,' said Mrs Stringer.

'You keep your nose out,' Luther said. 'This was nowt to do wi' women.'

'It's summat to do wi' our Bess,' his wife said. 'Your own daughter's young man an' you're doin' this to him.'

'Nay, don't blame me. There's nowt I could do about it if I wanted.'

'Which you don't,' said Bessie, her colour rising.

33

'I've said what I have to say.' And Luther retired behind his paper again.

'Well, I've summat to say now,' Bessie flashed. 'It doesn't matter what your flamin' union does to Bob. He's headin' for better things than t'shop floor an' bein' bossed about by a pack o' tuppence ha'penny workmen.'

'Shurrup, Bessie,' Bob muttered. 'There's no need to go into all that.'

'I think there is,' Bessie said. 'I think it's time me father wa' told a thing or two. Who does he think he is, anyway? I don't suppose you know,' she said to Luther, who was reading his paper with a studied show of not listening to her, ' 'at Bob's been takin' a course in accountancy at nights. An' I don't suppose you know that Mr Matthew Whittaker himself has heard about this an' that he's as good as promised Bob a job upstairs in the Costing Office if he does well in his exams. What do you think about that, eh?'

The paper slowly lowered to reveal Luther's face again. 'I'll tell you what I think about it,' he said. 'I think you'd better take that young feller out o' my house an' never bring him back again.' His voice began to rise as his feelings got the better of him. 'So he works because he doesn't agree wi' t' union policy, does he? He thinks we ought to have wage restraint, does he? He stuffs me up wi' that tale an' now you tell me he's anglin' for a job on t'staff. It wasn't his principles 'at made him go in yesterday, it wa' because he wanted to keep on t'right side o' t'management.'

'Calm yourself, Luther,' Mrs Stringer said. 'You'll have a stroke if you get so worked up.'

'I'll have a stroke if ever I see that . . . that blackleg in my house again,' Luther shouted.

'I shall marry him whether you like it or not,' Bessie said.

'Not at my expense, you won't.'

'C'mon, Bessie,' Bob said. 'Let's be off.'

'Aye, we'll go,' said Bessie. 'You'd better see if you can control him, Mother. He's yours. This one's mine.'

Bessie and Bob left the house and Mrs Stringer went to wash-up, leaving Luther pacing the living-room, muttering to himself. In a few moments he followed her into the kitchen, in search of an audience.

'Wage restraint,' he said. 'Think for yourself. Don't be led off like a flock o' sheep. Oh he knows how to think for hisself, that one does. You know, I half-admired him for sticking to his principles, even if I did think he was daft in the head. But that one's not daft. Not him. He's crafty. He's not botherin' hisself about wage restraint an' principle. He's wonderin' what Matthew'll think if he strikes wi' t'rest on us. He's wonderin' if Matthew mightn't get his own back by forgettin' that job he promised him. That's what he calls a fair boss. He knows bosses as well as' t'rest on us. Principle! He's no more principle than a rattlesnake . . .'

Mrs Stringer said nothing.

'Well, our Bessie can wed him if she likes. She'll go her own road in the end, an' she's too old to be said by me. But there's no need to plan on bringin' him here to live. They'll have to find some place of their own . . . An' what's more, I won't have you havin' 'em in the house when I'm out. You hear what I say, Agnes? You're to have no more to do wi' that young man.'

It was at this point that Mrs Stringer, who had not said a word so far, suddenly uttered a long drawn-out moan as of endurance taxed to its limit. 'O-o-oh! For heaven's sake, will you shut up!' And bringing a dinner plate clear of the soapy water she lifted it high in both hands and crashed it down on the tap.

Luther's jaw dropped as the pieces clattered into the sink. 'Have you gone daft?'

'I shall go daft if I hear you talk much longer.'

'That's a plate from t'best dinner service you've just smashed.'

'I know it is, an' I don't care. You can pay for it out o' that rise your union's gettin' you. As for me, I've had enough. I'm havin' my one-day strike tomorrow. I'm off to our Gertie's first thing an' I shan't be back till late.

You can look after yourself. Aye, an' talk to yourself, for all I care.'

'You're not feelin' badly, are you?' Luther said. 'What's come over you?'

'Principle,' Mrs Stringer said. 'Twenty-seven year of it, saved up.' And with that she walked out of the kitchen and left him.

Luther went back into the living-room and picked up his paper. He switched on the radio for the news and switched off immediately when he got the amplified roar of a pop group. He tried for some minutes to read the paper, and then threw it down and wandered out into the passage and stood at the foot of the stairs, looking up at the landing as though wondering what his wife was doing. He remained in that attitude for several minutes, and then, as though reaching a decision, or dismissing the problem as not being worth the worry, he reached for his cap and coat and left the house for the pub on the corner where he was sure to find someone who spoke his language.

Closing Time

By the time Halloran had backed his fancy and got out of
Mulholland's Betting Shop and gone along the road, the
landlord of the Greyhound, Jack Marshall, was shutting
his front door. Halloran shouted, 'Ey! Ey, Jack!' Marshall
looked round the door as Halloran crossed the road in a
stiff-legged run.

'Am I not in time for one?' Halloran asked, catching his
breath.

'Nay, Michael, it's gone twenty past three.'

'I was hoping to see Tommy Corcoran,' Halloran said.

'He was up and away half an hour ago. They've all
gone. And I'm closing.'

Halloran pulled at his long thin nose, his brow
wrinkling in thought.

'There's no harm in me comin' in for a minute. If I could
just see the telly for the three-thirty.'

The landlord hesitated, then stood aside. 'Come on,
then, before t'bobby sees you.'

'Sure, they can't object to a man lookin' at the telly.'

'They object to all sorts o' things on licensed premises.'

Halloran went into the big lounge bar where the television set stood high up on a shelf at one end of the long
counter. He watched as Marshall switched on and the
screen flickered into life. In a moment his eyes fell and
passed over the pump handles. His seeming to catch
everything in the tail of his gaze, as though his brain were
a fraction slow in registering what his eyes moved across,
gave him an appearance of slyness.

'Ah, you've got the . . . the towels on.'

'I have,' Marshall said. 'And they're not coming off.'

'Ah!' Halloran nodded several times. Then he held up a tentative hand, the thumb and forefinger an inch apart. 'Perhaps a . . . ?'

'You'll get me shot,' the landlord said. 'I expect you've spent all dinnertime at the Black Horse.'

'No, no.' Halloran shook his head. 'I haven't had a drop today. Honest.'

'I'll believe you, where thousands wouldn't,' Marshall said. 'All right. What's it to be?'

'A rum an' pep. You're a decent man, Jack . . . Did Tommy Corcoran ask after me at all?'

'Not that I know of. Was it summat special you had to see him about?'

'He thought there might be the chance of a job on the site.' Halloran took the glass the landlord placed on the bar counter and felt for his money. 'Will you, er . . . ?'

'No, thanks all the same, Michael. I've had me ration for this dinnertime.'

He put the coins in the till and gave Halloran his change.

'A job, eh? You're not going back to carryin' the hod at your age, are you?'

'Oh, I've still plenty of life in me,' Halloran said.

'Oh, aye, I don't doubt that.'

At fifty-five, Halloran, with a wife ten years younger than himself, had just fathered his eleventh child. With the dole and family allowances, plus various supplementary benefits, they managed to live in the periods when Halloran was out of work – periods which were now longer than those in which he was employed. Sometimes he would be technically in work but playing sick with one of his recurrent disabilities: his back, his chest, or his legs. His contempt matched that of others when discussing the work-shy who lived off social security and were kept by the dues and taxes of more conscientious men.

The landlord washed and polished glasses as the runners lined up for the three-thirty race.

'You've got summat on this, have you, Michael?'

'I have.'

'And what is it you fancy?'

Halloran held up a quietening hand as the commentator began to speak. Marshall shrugged and went back into the private quarters to have a word with his wife.

'Is there anybody still through there?'

'Only Michael Halloran. He popped in to watch the three-thirty.'

'He's not drinking, is he?'

'Only a small rum and pep.'

'You're daft, Jack, risking trouble with the police for a feller like Michael Halloran.'

'It's all right. If they come in, he's with me.'

'You'd think some of them had no homes to go to.'

'His must be a bit crowded.'

'Whose fault is that?'

'Aye, all right, then, don't get on. He'll be away in a minute.'

'You're the wrong type to keep a pub, Jack. You lean too much to your customers.'

'Don't talk so daft. How much drinking after time have you seen here? I run this place as well as anybody else could. A bit more interest from you 'ud be a help.'

'You know how I feel about it. You've never done. It's after half past three now. You'll be open again at six and you won't get to bed till one. What kind of life is that?'

'It's a pity you didn't say all this before we came.'

'I did, but you wouldn't listen.'

It was true. He'd known he was persuading her against her real wishes, but he'd persisted, hoping she would take to the life in time. Instead, she had become more bitter and dissatisfied than she had ever been. With their children grown up and gone away, Marshall had looked for something they could tackle together, which they could build on towards better things. His idea was to acquire experience here for the time when they could have their own business – perhaps a small hotel, or in some branch of catering. But to his wife they had gone from the voluntary bondage of the family to the enforced one of licensing hours and regulations, the need to be pleasant to people they didn't care for, and all the endless comings and goings of pub life. She had never cared for pubs. It was all beneath her.

Marshall looked at his watch. 'The race'll be over now. I'll get him out and finish clearing up.'

When he went back into the bar there was no sign of Halloran. Marshall switched off the television set and washed out Halloran's empty glass. He waited a while for Halloran to come back from the gents, then went to look for him. He was not there; nor, with the front door still bolted, was there any indication that he had left.

'Now, where the hell's he gone to?' he said out loud.

He took cloth and bucket and went round into the lounge to empty the ashtrays and wipe the tabletops. It was when he turned in the process of doing this to face the bar counter that he saw Halloran slumped there on the floor. Marshall went and crouched over him.

'Now then, Michael, what's all this about?'

His first impulse was to lift Halloran under the armpits and get him on to a chair; but when he saw that the man was unconscious and breathing in an odd, strained way, he straightened up and called along the passage to his wife.

'Nora! Nora! Come here, will you?'

'What's wrong?'

'Come here. Quick!'

She came at her own speed. 'What is it?'

'It's Halloran.'

She stretched up and leaned over the counter. 'Oh God! Is he drunk?'

'No, he's badly. He's collapsed. I think it's his heart.'

She came round. 'Has he complained about it at all?'

'He's complained about all manner of things. Half the time I didn't believe him.'

'Can't you bring him round?'

'Nay, I don't know how to deal with this. He needs expert attention.'

'Shall I ring for a doctor?'

'Better dial 999 for an ambulance. That'll be quicker.'

'They don't like that unless it's an emergency.'

'It is an emergency. He could be dying, for all we know. And bring me that travelling-rug and cushion out of the living-room. I daren't move him but I'd better wrap him up and keep him warm.'

The ambulance was at the door in six minutes, diverted from a scheduled call in the district by a wireless message.

'It looks like a coronary,' one of the two men said as they got Halloran on to a stretcher. 'Have you got his name and address?'

'Aye. Where will you take him?'

'The General. Has he got a wife?'

'Yes. I'll go round and tell her as soon as you've gone.'

He saw them out through the front door and watched the ambulance move off. His wife was in the lounge again when he went in. She held up a piece of paper.

'Is this anything important?'

'It's a betting slip. Where did you find it?'

'On the floor, where he'd been lying.'

'I'll see to it.' He folded the slip and tucked it into his waistcoat pocket.

'Are you going to see the wife now?'

'I ought to. Isn't it that stone-built cottage at the far end of Furness Street?'

'Don't ask me. You'd better watch out for a horde of kids.'

'Aye. Will you finish off in here for me while I'm gone?'

She looked round reluctantly.

'There's not much to do,' he said.

'All right.'

Don't bloody force yourself, he thought in a spasm of temper. Always, in everything, working against the grain. He went out through the back door to the car in the yard.

Passing Mulholland's Betting Shop on the way he

remembered the slip and stopped. He went in and showed it to the clerk.

'Is there anything to draw on this?'

The clerk looked it up in his ledger. 'I'll say there is. Didn't you hear the result?'

'No. It's not mine, you see.'

'Oh. Wait a minute. Wasn't this bet placed by Michael Halloran?'

'That's right. He was taken ill in my pub and I found it afterwards. I'm on my way to see his wife.'

'I'm sorry to hear that. Is he bad?'

'We won't know till she phones the hospital.'

'They've taken him away, then?'

'Yes. If you'd rather I got his wife to come herself.'

'No, that's all right. You've got the slip. It'll be a nice surprise for Michael, when he hears about it.'

'You mean it's a sizeable win?'

'He had a fiver on "Rocky Road", an outsider. It came in at 33 to 1. A damn good job we laid it off.'

'Good heavens!'

'It'll maybe cheer his missis up as well.'

'I should think so!'

He found the Hallorans' house on a stretch of unmade road at the dead end of Furness Street. It stood on a patch of ground, littered with old sheds and a wired-in enclosure full of hens, by a now disused railway line. There were slates missing from the low sagging roof and it was possible only to guess what colour the last coat of paint had been. The woman who answered his knock had lingering signs of prettiness in her dark, nearly black eyes, and the set of her cheekbones. She carried a baby in her arms as she looked at him.

'Mrs Halloran? I'm Jack Marshall from the Greyhound. I've got a message about your husband.'

'Yes?'

'I'm afraid he's been taken ill.' He saw the fear spring at once into her eyes.

'Ill?'

'He collapsed in the pub. I thought it best to call

an ambulance. They've taken him to the Infirmary.'

Two children had appeared in the doorway now. They tugged at her skirt. 'What's wrong, Mam?' She spoke to them with a surprising gentleness, her gaze never leaving Marshall's face.

'This gentleman's come with a message about your father. He's not . . . ?' She shook her head slowly as though willing him to give a favourable answer.

'No, no. If you just give 'em a chance to see to him, and then ring up, you'll very likely find he's all right . . . There was something else . . . If I could come in for a minute . . .'

'All right.'

He followed her through the door into a big unkempt all-purpose room. The reek from some badly washed nappies drying on the brass rail of the guard round the hot fire caught at his throat and he swallowed hard, controlling a desire to retch.

'Your husband had a bet on a horse this afternoon. It came in at 33 to 1.' He took the bundle of fivers out of his pocket and put it on the table. 'A hundred and fifty-nine pounds, and some silver. Perhaps you'd like to count it.'

She barely glanced at it. He didn't think she could understand.

'It's a lot of money,' he said.

'I can't get out of the house just now,' she said. 'Maybe when my bigger ones get in from school . . . But there's still the baby. He has to be fed regular, and I'm givin' him the breast, y'see.' She bit her lower lip fretfully. 'Will I be able to see him, d'you think?'

'I'd telephone first,' Marshall said, 'just to see how he is.'

He suddenly realized that she was finding the problem insuperable.

'Would you like me to ring up myself a bit later on, then come back and tell you how he is?'

'Would you do that? It sounds like an awful trouble.'

'It's no trouble.'

One of the children, a boy of about three, pulled up

43

one side of his trousers and began to urinate on the flagstone floor in a corner.

'Kevin!' his mother said, softly reproachful. 'Don't you know better than that? What will the gentleman think? Go and get a cloth and wipe it up, now.'

'Oh, poor Michael,' she said then. 'I thought there was something wrong with him this morning, when he hardly touched the breakfast I cooked for him. He's not strong, y'know.'

Marshall turned at the door. 'I'll pop back later, then, and tell you the news. And I'd put that somewhere safe.'

'What?' She glanced over her shoulder. 'Oh, yes.'

The bigger of the children had climbed on to a chair and was setting out the notes singly in rows across the top of the table.

'D'you think you could pass on a message to him when you telephone?'

'I'll see.'

'Will you tell him he's not to worry, an' I'll be over to see him as soon as I can.'

'I'll do that.'

Marshall took several very deep breaths on his way back to the car, filling his lungs with cold fresh air.

His wife was vacuuming in one of the bedrooms. She came down when she heard the car, and the back door slam.

'Did you find her, then?'

'Aye, I found her. You know that betting slip you picked up? Halloran had backed a 33 to 1 winner. I called in at Mulholland's and took the money round to his wife. A hundred and fifty-nine quid.'

'Good gracious! Wasn't he watching the racing when he collapsed?'

'Yes, he was.'

'You don't think the shock could have done it to him?'

'Nay, I don't know.'

'I expect his wife would be pleased to see all that money.'

'She took no notice of it. She was more bothered about Halloran.'

'Oh? Well, that's fitting, anyway.'

'All the same, it's a lot of money.'

'Yes. It'll come in useful with all that lot to feed and clothe. Twelve, is it?'

'Eleven.'

'What's one more or less when you've got so many? How do they manage with them all? He hardly ever works, yet he drinks and gambles. I'll bet it's a right muckhole. Isn't it?'

'Oh, aye,' Marshall said.

'And him. What she'll have to put up with him.'

Marshall gave a short exasperated snort of laughter. He looked at her, throwing out his hands.

'They're as happy as pigs in shit,' he said.

'Such *language!*' his wife said.

Estuary

'It comes in fast, doesn't it?' Parker said. He sat with his large soft-skinned hands holding his coffee cup at a table in the window of the café over the confectioner's shop and watched the rippling grey line of the bore as it swept silently up the channels between the low muddy sand-banks in the river-mouth.

It was the first time that one of his mid-morning visits to the café had given him such a good view of the tide at the most impressive stage of its sweep into the estuary. The first time, also, since he plodded up the lino-covered stairs three days ago, that he had addressed any words of conversation to the grey-haired, bespectacled wait-ress who stood beside him now with ballpen poised over her bill-pad.

He was a hefty young man, crouching bulkily, shoul-ders hunched, over the flimsy table. But his skin had the pallor of a recent illness and he looked as though he had lost some weight.

'There won't be a bit of land to be seen in half an hour,' the waitress said. 'It fills up quickly once it starts.'

Parker saw how the bore, its sweep broken by the concrete feet of the railway viaduct, encircled and isolated the smooth mounds of dark river sand.

'It'd be an easy thing to get cut off, I reckon.'

'They've to fetch people out every year,' the waitress said.

'Don't they see the danger?'

'Some people never see danger till it's too late,' the

46

waitress said. 'Of course, it isn't all that bad at this time of year. But you should see it in the spring. We get some real tides then. If anybody gets in then they don't stand much chance, I can tell you. They get caught in the current under the bridge and you can't get to them in time. We had a man drowned there this year.'

There was unconscious satisfaction in her voice: an involuntary touch of pride in this dangerous phenomenon on her doorstep.

Parker drained his cup and felt for some money.

'It was two vanilla slices, wasn't it?'

'Yes, two.'

He was reminded once again, with a pang, of his mother as the waitress made out the bill and laid it by his plate.

'Pay downstairs at the desk, sir, if you please.'

He had always had a sweet tooth and every day when the local baker had delivered his tray of cakes and pastries to the little general shop, Parker's mother had kept her sharp eyes and tongue on guard. 'You just keep your hands off them vanilla slices, Bernard my lad. I'm watching you and they're all accounted for.'

He put a threepenny bit on the table and went downstairs. When he had settled his bill at the counter he walked across the narrow promenade to the river wall and sat down on a bench to watch the tide.

A few small boats, grounded on the shore, moved and eventually floated as the water curled under and lifted them. A train rattled across the viaduct and Parker saw the anonymous faces of the passengers as they were carried over the deepening water swirling about the legs of the structure. The sun glistened on the water, and down on the narrowing shore a child laughed in a sudden spasm of joy. The menace of the tide fascinated Parker and held him there while the sandbanks slowly submerged and the estuary became an unbroken stretch of water, calm enough on the surface but current-corrupted beneath, from a few yards below his feet to the distant line of the far shore; and it was not until the noon sun clanged brassily off the water into his eyes and he stood up to walk back to his lodgings that his mind sank again into contemplation of the emptiness of his life.

It was a small and cosy life he had lived with his mother in the years since his father died. Unlike his father he had felt no pull from the world outside the little shop with the house behind it. He had never much cared for his father, whom he vaguely felt had held him in some contempt, and when his father died he had drawn closer than ever to his mother in an understanding where monosyllables and gestures conveyed almost all they wished to say. And he was content. There seemed no reason why anything should change. He never thought about it. But then he had contracted pneumonia and while he was in the period of crisis, fighting for his own life, his mother had two strokes in quick succession, the second one finishing her. They told him nothing until they felt him strong enough to take the news, and even so it was not until he went back to the closed shop and the empty house that full realization of it all broke into his stupefied mind.

He would be wise to go away for a while, the doctor said. Have a complete change; go somewhere quiet and stroll in the sun; sort himself out and come to terms with his new life. So he had come here to sit on the narrow promenade or drink coffee and eat vanilla slices in the café over the shop while the tide ran into the estuary from the sea.

Every day Parker came down the hill from his lodgings to watch the tide. He would have liked to explore the country inland but he still tired easily, and only during the second week did he venture along the river path that led off the promenade and gave on to a tree-lined stretch of shore out of sight of the village. Here he found that he could sit, away from people, in an almost mindless contemplation of the river in which the pain of the change in his life was curiously dulled. And here, on the third day, he saw the swimmer.

Men quite often bathed inshore off the promenade, but

this head bobbed far out where the sea ran at its strongest into the basin. Parker stood there for some time, watching the tiny distant movements of the swimmer in the waste of water. Then he crunched slowly across the shingle to the pile of clothing which lay just above the high-water line. There seemed to be only one garment there: a bathrobe of soft red-and-white striped towelling. He could also see now, through the trees, a white-stuccoed house with a flat parapeted roof. When he turned back to the river it took him a moment to locate the swimmer and he saw that the man was making for the shore, swimming with strong sure strokes. Some minutes later he became aware that the swimmer wore a bathing-cap and was not a man but a woman.

He wanted to move away but curiosity kept him there until she reached the shallows and stood up to walk out. Then it was too late to go without speaking. As she came towards him, removing the rubber cap and shaking her head to free the short dark hair, he said awkwardly, 'I was just thinking you might be in trouble.'

Black, expressionless eyes met his briefly. 'No, no trouble.'

'They said it was dangerous to swim any way out.'

'It's all right if you're a strong swimmer,' the woman said.

Though older than himself, she was still young: about thirty, Parker thought. As she dropped the cap and lifted her hands to her hair she stretched herself tall, rising slightly on her toes. Her whole body gave an impression of flatness in its width of hips and the smooth hardly developed curves of her breasts, which reminded Parker later of the gentle mounds of sand in the estuary, the cold rigid nipples like pebbles under the wet clinging skin of her black one-piece swimsuit. Her face was dark and sallow-skinned, and her black eyes seemed never to lose that constant inscrutable stare.

She took cigarettes from a pocket of the robe, offering them to Parker and, when he refused, lighting one for herself. Then she put on the robe and began to rub

49

herself dry, the smoke from the cigarette between her pale lips making her narrow her eyes.

'It's the only exciting thing round here,' she said suddenly. 'Everything else is half dead.'

'I was wondering if I ought to go for help,' Parker said.

'It would have been too late,' she said. 'They couldn't have got a boat to me in time.'

He looked after her when, a few moments later, she walked away with an easy, graceful swing of her body towards the trees, and she came into his mind from time to time during the rest of the day. Until, when he was undressing for bed, he found himself wondering why he should think of her. He had never needed women in his little world and, apart from a momentary flicker of sexual curiosity about some girl in the shop or a face glimpsed briefly on the television screen, thoughts of them had not troubled him. Yet he thought of this one, the flat body, the undeveloped breasts, and unfathomable black eyes coming to him time and again. Always he saw her lifting herself out of the water as he had seen her that morning, and it seemed to him that she had become inextricably associated with his thoughts of the tide and its fascination for him.

He drifted into a heavy, dream-laden sleep in which he found himself down in the estuary, walking on one of the sandbanks at night. He became aware of the bore, silver in the moonlight, sweeping silently along the channels on either side and in sudden fear he turned one way and another, to find water all round him. He began to run across one of the channels, feeling the water deepening round his legs until all at once there was nothing under his feet and he was thrashing madly, in panic, trying to keep his head and shouting at the top of his voice, 'I can't swim. I can't swim.' The woman's voice answered him. 'It's all right if you're a strong swimmer.' He had a sense of someone near him, and then he began to shout again as a terrible pressure forced him under the surface. The water flooded his lungs and the blood beat in his head until he thought his brain would burst.

He was crouching near the foot of the bed when he woke, the clothes spilling over on to the floor. He dragged them up round him and lay shivering in the dark, his body clammy with sweat, his heart beating with sickening force.

Behind the house where Parker was staying were fields trailing off into common land which ran up into the wooded headland that cut off the view of the bay and the open sea. For some time he had felt a desire to watch the full sweep of the tide as it rolled in across the sands. The rim of the headland looked to be no more than a mile and a half away, and on a hot afternoon towards the end of the second week he set out to walk up there.

Crossing the common, climbing steadily all the time, he felt the sun on his back and he took off his jacket and carried it over his arm. By the time he reached the edge of the trees he was tired and thirsty. His thighs ached and his armpits were soaked in sweat. The distance to the headland, foreshortened in the view from his bedroom window, was twice his original estimate and it was only the thought that it would be cooler under the trees which kept him going forward. The paths he had seen seemed to lead away from his objective and he had ignored them, climbing in what he judged to be a direct line to the headland across the rough tussocky grass. Now, at the edge of the wood, his view of the higher ground cut off, he faced the way he wanted to go and walked straight in under the trees.

Five minutes later he seemed to be lost, and looking back he could not make out the way he had come. He was entirely alone and even the occasional bird-calls seemed a part of the silence which surrounded him. When he saw two sets of initials cut into the trunk of a silver birch he reached out to them as if for reassurance. RF–GL: friends who had been this way, stood on this same spot, ten years ago. Or, more likely, lovers, welcoming the solitude of the wood. Parker gazed pensively at the letters as his relaxed fingers traced their outline.

He went on, hoping for some break in the trees which would allow him to get his bearings, and came presently into an open space that turned out to be a trap of grass-covered brambles into which he blundered and entangled his legs, falling forward and slashing his hands and face before he pulled himself clear and lay flat on the ground, his heart hammering, his breath coming in short painful gasps.

As his body relaxed he closed his eyes and slept for a time, waking with dry hard lips and a raging desire for water. He got on to his feet and clutched at a tree as the wood reeled before his eyes in a blur of sunlight and shadow. When he felt steadier he began to move down through the trees. It was rough going: he clambered down steep banks and skirted impenetrable thickets, not knowing where he was going but always heading downhill, his throat parched, his head swimming from over-exertion. He had done too much, he kept telling himself; a lot too much. He was a fool for having taken it on. His mother would— No, not his mother. He stopped abruptly in his thinking at the inescapable fact that his mother would never rebuke him again. There was no-one to rebuke him. He could do as he liked. His behaviour and his welfare were matters for himself now. He was on his own. 'Are them shoes wet, Bernard? Changed your clothes. You're asking for pneumonia delivering orders in them wet things.' Never again. She'd always said he had a stubborn, foolhardy streak that he'd inherited from his father . . .

Ten minutes of downhill stumbling and scrambling brought him, almost exhausted, first to signs of tree-felling and then a vehicle-width track with the impressions of heavy tyres in the soft black earth. Now the going was easier. He caught glimpses of the river through the trees and then the glare of sunlight on the white walls of a house. The sun caught him again as he emerged from the shade of the trees and he wondered if he dare ask at the house for water. He shrank from it, but he had never known such a thirst. Still thinking of it, he went along under a tall cedarboard fence until he came to a gate. He was standing there in indecision when the woman he had watched swimming in the estuary two days before came up the lane from the direction of the shore.

Her bare feet were in rope sandals. She wore a pale blue cotton beach-dress, tied at the waist and reaching halfway down her thighs.

Parker saw as she came nearer that her hair was damp, and he knew she had been swimming. For some reason the knowledge started small fluttering tremors of excitement in the bottom of his stomach.

She looked at him without recognition. 'Was there something you wanted?'

'I was up the hill,' Parker stammered. 'I got lost . . . I was wondering if I could have a drink of water.'

He stood aside as she reached for the latch of the gate. Her gaze rested on him and he felt a flush of colour spreading up from his neck.

'You'd better come in.'

He followed her to the kitchen door and waited while she ran a tumbler of water and brought it to him on the step. He drank it straight down without stopping. It took his breath away and he gasped as he lowered the glass from his lips.

'I was ready for that.'

She took the tumbler from him. 'Don't you feel well? You look pale, and there's blood on your face.'

'I got lost,' Parker told her again. 'Up the hill, there. Then I fell headfirst into some brambles.'

'You look done in,' the woman said. 'Look, why not come in and sit down for a while?'

'Oh, I'll be all right now,' Parker said. 'I feel better already.'

She asked him if he was staying in the village. Then, 'You really ought to come in and sit down. You don't want to walk any more till you've had a rest.'

He was uncomfortable under her direct expressionless gaze. He said, 'Well, just for a minute, then. I don't want to put you out.'

'Don't be silly,' she said, turning into the house. 'Come on.'

He was conscious again of the grace of her movements as she led him through the kitchen and into a long, airy lounge with big windows looking out towards the river.

'Sit down,' she said. 'You'll feel better after a rest.'

Parker lowered himself on to the edge of an armchair. 'I don't want to get in your way.'

'I'm not going anywhere,' she said. She put her hand on his shoulder and pressed him back into the soft upholstery.

'Sit back,' she said. 'Be comfortable.'

Her complete self-possession astonished Parker. He had never met anyone quite like her before. But he rested his head back gratefully and looked round the room, hearing the chink of a glass behind him, then her voice saying, 'Here, drink this. It'll set you up.'

He took the glass she held out to him.

'It's brandy,' she said as he looked at it. 'More pep in it than water.'

'I don't reckon to—' he began, and she said, 'Drink it up. It'll do you good.'

She sat on the arm of a chair opposite him as he sipped from the glass.

'Better?'

He nodded, feeling the fire of the brandy in his throat.

'Have you walked a long way?'

'I set off for the top,' Parker said, 'but I got lost and came down again.'

She nodded. 'It's easy to lose your sense of direction round here.'

'I wanted to watch the tide coming in,' Parker said. 'But I took too much on.'

'Too much? It's not far if you know the way. Aren't you used to walking?'

She made statements and asked questions in the same flat, incurious voice, as though she was concerned only in asking and not with the answers he gave her. And the

54

black eyes seemed to support this; for though they never left him for more than a few seconds, they rested so dispassionately on him they seemed to be occupied with some aspect that was of him yet somehow not of him. It struck him that she was regarding him with the withdrawn composure of someone contemplating an object.

'I've been poorly, you see,' he told her. 'I'm supposed to be resting and getting myself well again, not knocking myself up.'

'You've been ill?' Her eyes moved again to his face.

'I had pneumonia.'

'Bad?'

'I nearly died,' Parker said. 'I was lucky.'

Surprisingly now, she began to admonish him, as though she had some personal interest in his welfare . . . 'You need somebody to stop you doing silly things. Are you married?'

Parker shook his head. 'No. I lived with my mother, but she died.'

He was ill at ease again. He looked into his glass, then lifted it to take another sip of the brandy. It was doing him good. He felt a lot better already.

'What made you come to this place? Have you been before?'

'No, but I wanted somewhere quiet and it was recommended to me.'

She was at the window now, looking out, her back to him. He felt easier.

'It's quiet, all right,' she said. 'I've lived here for three years. Since I got married. I was on the stage before that.' She spun round to face him. 'Did you guess I'd been on the stage? Could you tell?'

'I thought there was something about you,' Parker said.

She nodded. 'You can always tell. It stamps you, being on the stage.'

She went into a long story about herself, about her career before her marriage, telling him of the shows she had appeared in, the towns she had visited, the people she had met.

55

Until, in a break in her monologue, Parker said, 'What made you give it up if you liked it so much?'

'Liked it?' She gazed at him as though looking straight through him to something beyond him. Then she shrugged. 'I suppose it's all right if you've got what it takes. But there was no future in the kind of stuff I was doing. It was cheap-jack stuff. It's all right if you can get on, but I knew I never could. I hadn't got what it takes. I hadn't the figure, for one thing.'

Parker looked at her in the short beach-dress, at the light tan on her limbs. He said diffidently, 'I think you've got nice legs.'

'Oh, they're all right,' she said indifferently. 'But I've no bust.' She ran her hands down over her flat breasts, posing in the sunlight flooding through the big window. 'And I'm not pretty. And my skin's sensitive. You might not think so, but it is. I couldn't stand all that make up.'

Parker drank off the last of his brandy.

'Do you want another drink?' she asked him. 'Some more brandy, or some whisky?'

'No, thanks. That was all right.'

'A cigarette, then?'

Parker said no. 'I don't smoke.'

'Haven't you ever smoked?'

'No, I never got the habit.'

She took a cigarette for herself from a chrome-plated box on the low occasional table and lit it before sitting on the cushioned windowseat and swinging up her feet to stretch full length her long flat body and graceful legs. She puffed inexpertly on the cigarette, without inhaling.

Anxious not to outstay his welcome, Parker was gathering words of leavetaking, when she spoke again. 'I left the stage for security,' she said. 'That's what everybody wants, isn't it?'

'I suppose so,' Parker said.

'Yes, but it's dull,' she said. 'It's so dull I could scream.' She turned her head towards him for a moment. 'I'm talking a lot, aren't I?'

'I don't mind,' Parker said. 'I think mebbe I should be going, though.'

'Miles was married before, you know,' she said. 'He'd been married a long time. He's nearly sixty. They don't like me round here. They remember his first wife. She was in on everything. Miles is disappointed that I don't mix more. But I've tried to be friendly and they don't like me. I can feel it. They think I hooked Miles, but they're wrong. He was mad about me. He begged me to marry him. I was quite a time making up my mind.'

Parker sat forward in his chair and put down the empty glass. He took his mind off the woman by concentrating on the effect of the brandy. It had done him a power of good. An early night tonight and he'd be all fixed up.

'We don't go out much,' the woman was saying. 'There's nothing to do here: no shops or theatres. But Miles doesn't mind. He plays the gramophone when he's at home.' She reached down and slid open a cupboard under the window-seat, revealing a neat row of records in their sleeves. 'Look at all those. That's all he does besides fishing. All he does: play records. Nothing lively, though; all dull stuff: Beethoven, Handel, Mozart. The duller they are, the more Miles likes them . . .'

'Is that why you swim in the river?' Parker said.

'It's the only exciting thing round here,' she said. 'And I can only do that when Miles isn't at home. He's furious if he knows I've done it. He lost a boy in the bay once. He's never got over it. It was his only child. He talks about it sometimes when he's feeling sentimental. Then it makes me feel good to know I can beat it.'

Parker got up. He didn't know where to put his hands.

'I ought to be going.'

She went out with him and at the gate he thanked her again. 'Saved my life, I reckon,' he said, forcing a tight grin.

'You can come again, if you like,' she said. 'You could sit out in the garden and rest. You're too pale; you need sun.'

'I go home Saturday,' Parker told her.

'Well, come tomorrow. See if you can get your face red to go home with. You can't go back looking so pale.'

There was nobody to notice, anyway, Parker thought. He said, 'I could come in the afternoon, I suppose.'

'Yes, do that. Come after lunch.'

She showed him the shortest way back to the village and he left carrying with him the image of her running her hands over her body in the sunlight, the excitement fluttering in him as he thought of this and the flood of talk released in the extremity of her boredom. There was no need to go back, he told himself. He could decide tomorrow.

'Would you like another drink?' she asked, and Parker started. The silence since either of them had spoken had been so long that, dozing himself, he had thought her asleep. There was a tray with tumblers and a vacuum jug of iced lime-juice in the shade of the trees nearby.

Parker said, 'No, thanks,' and lifted himself on to his elbows on the rug. He had been in the garden for nearly an hour now. The sun was hot again and his shirt clung damply under his arms.

After lunch he had sat for a time in the garden of the cottage before setting out across the village. He entered the grounds of the house by the main gate, walking up the driveway and mounting the shallow steps to press the bell by the front door. There was no reply and he rang again, wondering if she had forgotten her invitation; forgotten him, even, as soon as he had gone from her sight.

The house was quiet in the strong sunlight; deeply quiet, as though life had abandoned it, leaving it clean, preserved, but dead. It would be like one of those fantastic stories you sometimes read, he thought, if somebody else came to the door and told him they'd never heard of the woman. It struck him then that he did not know her name, and she had never asked his. He came down the steps again and walked with an increasing feeling of unreality round the side of the house to a gate in the tall cedar fence which shut off the garden and the back of the house. He opened it and went through, starting across the flagged area to the kitchen door before he saw her, lying face down on a travelling-rug by a border of flowering shrubs at the far end of the lawn.

She became aware of him before he was half-way to her.

'I thought you'd decided not to come,' she said. She raised herself on her elbows as he approached. The dark look flickered on to his face, then away again as she relaxed as before, with her face on her arms.

She was wearing a bathing-costume: not the one he had seen her swimming in, but a very brief two-piece of soft dark red wool.

'I rested for a bit,' Parker said.

'Isn't that what you were supposed to do here?' she said, and Parker thought she sounded like a petulant lover who had been kept waiting; not someone whom he had known only a few days; with whom he had exchanged only a few casual words before yesterday.

'I suppose so,' he said.

He stood looking down at her, at the sallow skin of her neck and the broadness of her back with the straight spinal gully between firm pads of flesh. When she didn't speak again he dropped his jacket and sat down beside her on the rug, resting his weight on one arm.

'I was just thinking how nice a cold drink would be,' she said then. 'I'll get some in a minute . . .'

Now, after the long silence, she said. 'I don't know how you can bear all those clothes. You should have brought some trunks and changed in the house.'

'I haven't got any,' Parker told her. 'I can't swim.'

'I could teach you in a week,' she said. 'But you're going home tomorrow, aren't you?'

'Yes,' Parker said. 'Tomorrow.'

'What do you do at home?'

'I've got a little shop: grocery.'

'Does it pay its way?'

'It does pretty fair . . . Course, there's only me to keep out of it now.'

There in the hot sunlight he was all at once mourning for his mother again, knowing that he was near the time when he must go home and face day-to-day existence without her. He had avoided making plans, as though unable to face the inevitable. Now he would be forced to think about it: about the housework and help in the shop; about the loneliness.

'You'll have to find yourself a girl,' the woman said. 'Get married.'

Just like that, Parker thought. It was the obvious thing. But the very thought of taking a wife into his life filled him with dread. And who could it be?

She had turned her head so that she could see him.

'Don't you bother with girls much?' she said, and Parker made an awkward, bashful movement of his hand without speaking.

'Somebody will take you in hand,' she said. 'There'll be somebody with her eye on you now.'

'I don't think so,' Parker said.

'You don't know much about women.'

'You're right there,' Parker said.

Her eyes were on him in one of those long moments of contemplation that so filled him with awkwardness and a feeling of inadequacy. He plucked at the cropped grass. What was he doing here, anyway? After nearly two weeks of being alone, looking at the river, thinking about home, he was here in a private garden with this strange, bored, restless woman. And she was leading the way at every step, spinning out of her boredom a web of excitement which gripped him now as it had from the first.

'The sun's moving round,' she said, taking her gaze off him. 'We ought to be up on the roof.'

'The roof?' he said stupidly.

'Yes. We can lie in the sun longer up there. That's what it's meant for.'

She sprang up and held out her hand. 'Come on.'

60

Parker allowed himself to be led across the lawn and into the house. The way to the roof lay up thickly carpeted stairs and along a corridor with closed white-painted doors. At the end of the corridor Parker followed the woman up another short flight of steps to a door which opened out into the sunlight.

At once he felt acutely exposed standing there on top of the house. He looked at the woman, who was at the rail surmounting the low parapet, gazing out at the river. She beckoned him and he went and stood beside her.

'Look,' she said, 'it's coming in.'

The view was better than any he had had before. From here he could see part of the bay and the low grey line of the sea, thrusting its foaming fringe before it deep into the river channels, and as he watched he felt the woman's fingers entwine themselves in his. There was a surprising strength in their grip, but it seemed to Parker that she was hardly conscious of him, all her concentration focused on the sweep of the tide. He wondered what was in her mind as she looked out there minute after minute, and all at once it came to him that she was afraid of the sea and he trembled slightly, feeling the heat and tension of her body against his forearm.

At last she released his hand and turned away to sink down on a large airbed which lay inflated on the flat roof. She lay with her face hidden from him. It was as though she had forgotten him.

Parker got down beside her in a silence that grew into minutes. He said at length, 'Are you asleep?'

'No . . . There's a bottle of suntan lotion somewhere about. Will you rub some into my back?'

Parker found the lotion and poured some into his hands. He held them poised over her back, unable to touch her until she said, 'Can't you find it?'

'Yes, I've got it.'

'Go on, then,' she said. 'Don't be shy.'

Parker flushed. He knelt beside her and laid his hands on her back. He began to work the lotion into her skin, the movement of flesh and muscle under his hands transmitting itself to him in slow mounting waves of excited feeling. When his fingers touched the string holding the upper half of her costume she said, 'Unfasten it.'

He pulled at the bow and parted the two halves of cord.

'You have smooth strong hands,' the woman said, 'I could fall asleep with you doing that.'

She stretched her limbs indolently, then relaxed again under the pressure of his touch. Again a feeling of being exposed came over Parker.

'Can't anybody see us up here?'

'Nobody,' the woman said. 'We're as private as if we were inside four walls. Sometimes I sunbathe in the nude up here, but Miles doesn't like it. He's very prudish, really. When he sees me like that it reminds him of when I was on the stage. He was on a night out with some business acquaintances and he came back three more times in the same week. He wanted me to leave the stage straight away, but I wouldn't throw up everything for him. I told you I was a long time making up my mind. He followed me to other places. He told me I'd the most exciting body he'd ever seen. But he forgot about his heart and that he wasn't a boy any longer.'

'You can't stay young for ever,' Parker said.

'You don't know anything about it, do you?' she said. 'You live your own life in your own little world, among people you've known for years . . .'

'I know what it's like to be lonely,' Parker said.

'What is it like?'

'I reckon it's something you've got to get used to.'

'You never get used to it,' the woman said. 'The most you can do is find moments when it goes away.'

Parker was looking at her right hand which rested, fingers slightly open, on the blue airbed, and noticing for the first time that the little finger was curiously malformed. The sight of that twisted finger on the small and otherwise well-shaped hand aroused in him a feeling he had never known before. He did not know how to deal with this strange compassionate feeling except by putting his hand on her back again and moving it over her skin as though lightly applying more oil. But there was a difference in its touch, and under its new tender urgency the woman shuddered, then turned over without speaking in a quick movement that exposed to him for a moment the naked front of her body before she reached out to pull him down into the bruising ferocity of her kiss. The nails of one hand dug into his shoulder and the light fluttering gasp of her breath was on his face as she drew away to speak to him.

'Now,' she said, 'Be very quick.'

He was nothing. He knew it through the flare of his response. Something the sea would use and discard. He thought it in the fleeting second before she took him, unresisting, plunging down with her into the vortex of her frenzy.

In the morning, his bag packed, Parker went back to look at the house. He had no words for the woman: no more than yesterday when he had left her as she slept in the sun. But something drew him back there. A car stood in the driveway, a large black saloon with dusty bodywork. He looked at it as he passed and went on without stopping.

The train was not busy and he found an empty compartment and settled himself by the window. As they swung out on the viaduct, the village falling away behind, Parker looked down the shoreline for the last glimpse of the white house through the trees. But there was nothing to see: nothing but the estuary, empty now, the smooth sandbanks drying in the sun, the river and its minor channels winding placidly out into the bay; free for a time of the deep dark treachery of the tide . . .

He thought about the woman often in the months that followed, and the memory of her brought a vague half-longing that sank him in moods of dreamy discontent. It was in one of these periods that he became engaged to the small plump slow-moving girl with the deep, tolerant laugh who had answered his advertisement for help; and since there was no reason to wait, he married her quickly and took her to live in the little house behind the shop. She was a good wife to him, and as the warmth and solid contentment of his new life enfolded him, the woman became increasingly dreamlike and remote until there came a time when he did not think of her any more.

Love and Music

Popping into the lounge bar of The Wheatsheaf just before lunch that Saturday morning, I was surprised to see Sam Skelmanthorpe sitting behind the bottom half of a pint and lighting up the room with the full glory of his scarlet tunic.

'Chalk that up to me, George,' he called to the landlord as I ordered my own half-pint of bitter; and once served, I went over, glass in hand, to join him.

'Contest today?' I asked him after a brief exchange of greetings.

'Wedding,' Sam said. 'Just got back.'

'Somebody important?'

'Important to us,' he said. He took a pull at his glass. 'Have you never seen a full brass band at a wedding?'

I said no, I hadn't. 'A lovely sight,' Sam said. 'And when they play it brings tears to your eyes. Better than any organ. Lovely.'

If there's a man who likes to tell the tale it's Sam Skelmanthorpe; but you have to work him round to it gently. And a little while later, when he was comfortably settled behind a fresh pint, with his pipe drawing well, he began to tell me all about it.

I don't suppose you know Dave Fothergill and Tommy Oldroyd, do you? Sam said. Well, they're two lads in the band. Young chaps, real pals. They've known one another right from the time their mothers took 'em to the clinic together as bairns; and before that, even, because their families lived on'y three doors apart down Royd's

Lane and there wasn't much more than twenty-four hours between them being born. You might say they were thrown together right from the start, and that's the way they carried on. They went to school together – and when you're young, y'know, you can change your pals as easy as changing your shirt.

But not Dave and Tommy. They stuck like glue.

We allus used to say it'd take a woman to come between 'em, and that's how it happened. Even then we were a bit surprised.

They took an interest in the band very early on, and soon they were nattering their dads to get 'em an instrument apiece. So their dads brought 'em to see the committee. We have one or two instruments that we lend out to learners and we said we'd fix 'em up, seeing as how they were so keen. We allus try to encourage young lads, y'know. Brass banding isn't what it used to be when I was a lad. What with all this television and radio, all this entertainment laid on, there isn't the interest in learning an instrument, some road.

Anyway, they both had to have the same instrument, o' course, and they picked the cornet as being to their liking. And old Jess Hodgkins, our conductor, offered to give 'em a few lessons just to put 'em into the way o' things.

Now they soon showed a bit o' capability and Jess used to talk about 'em at practices. 'I've two right good lads yonder,' he used to say, 'and do ye know, I'm blessed if I can tell which is t'best between 'em!' They kept on getting better, and when they could hold their end up a bit, we took 'em into the band. By the time they were sixteen or seventeen they were sharing the solo parts between 'em and we knew that we'd two o' the best young cornet players in Yorkshire. And we began to get a bit windy, I can tell you, because by the time young lads start working these days they're pining for the bright lights and pastures new, as they say. And we were a bit scared that one o' the big bands, like Fairey or t'Dyke might be hearing of 'em and snapping 'em up. Not that we'd have stood in their way, mind you; but they were two such grand players that they all but made our band, and we couldn't bear the thought o' losing 'em.

But as it turned out, they seemed well settled. When they left school they took to farming with old Withers, as keeps that place on Low Road, and this seemed to suit 'em nicely. They played engagements round about with any band that was short o' men, and they even had offers to go and play with jazz bands in Cressley and suchlike places. But they weren't having any o' that. No jungle music for them, they said. They were stopping where they could play some *real* stuff.

Well, all this was fine for us. But we all knew that one thing was sure to take 'em away and split 'em up, and this was their National Service. But you know, they went up together, they served together, and they came back together. And when we asked 'em how they'd managed it, they just grinned in that quiet way they both have and said it'd take more than the Army to split *them* up.

Well, I reckon you've guessed, it did. It took a lass. And a town lass at that.

Seeing as they wouldn't be away all that long, Withers had decided not to hire another man. He set a landgirl on. And no sooner had Dave and Tommy got back to work than the trouble started. Give credit where it's due – it was Short Fred, our librarian, who first spotted what was going on; and he used to come up to the band-room and tell us how both Dave and Tommy were making sheep's eyes at this lass; and how she was making up first to one then the other.

What I should tell you here is that neither of 'em to our knowledge had ever shown any interest in lasses afore; but this Cynthia was a sly bit. She made out she was a music lover, and that she'd heard 'em play. Find a man's weak spot, they say, don't they? Well, she found both Dave and Tommy's there. She had 'em danglin' straight away. Not satisfied with one, she had to set one off against the other by telling each of 'em, when the other wasn't there, that he was the finest player she'd ever heard.

67

One of the nicest things about Dave and Tommy up to this time was that there'd never been a breath of jealousy between 'em; but after a bit of Cynthia's tactics they started giving one another funny looks. In the end they gave up coming to practices, and word got about that they weren't speaking.

Well, this was a bit of a caper. I mean, it was the last thing anybody expected. And here we were with a full programme of summer concerts and our two best men behaving like bairns. We couldn't reckon it up at all. We studied it all roads, and we spent a lot o' time talking about it when we should have been practising. We sent Jack Thomas, our secretary, down to see 'em, and he came away with a flea in his ear. So there was nothing else we could do. I mean, folk have been getting into that kind of trouble ever since the Garden of Eden and the best thing to do is leave 'em to come round on their own. But that didn't alter the fact that we shouldn't sound so good without 'em, and we brooded about it.

Then one Thursday night both Dave and Tommy rolled into the band-room and sat down in their places. They didn't say much to nobody and not a word to one another. And when the practice was over they packed their instruments and walked off without stopping for a dust-slaker in the Fox and Ferret like they'd allus done before. We couldn't reckon this up, either. It left us with summat else to speculate about.

The same thing happened Sunday morning. In they walked, said nowt to nobody, did their playing, and walked out again. But after, Fred gave us a bit of news. Cynthia was leaving the farm. We were sure this had some bearing on it, and before long, what with odd bits of talk and gossip, we'd pieced it together, and the idea was this. They were both fed up with one another interfering with their courting, and still this Cynthia wouldn't plump for either of 'em. Well, it was being a music lover, like, that had first attracted her to 'em, so she said, and they both knew they'd be doing a bit o' showing off at our first concert, so they'd fixed up for her to come and hear them and make up her mind between them after.

In the week or two left before the concert they practised like mad, and folks used to hear music coming from down Royd's Lane at all hours of day and night. It got so bad towards the end that the bobby had to have a walk down and tell 'em that all this midnight triple-tonguing constituted a public nuisance, and they'd better tone it down – or else!

I remember that the Sunday after Whit was a lovely day. We hadn't another like it all summer. We hired a bus as usual to take us and the tackle down to the park, and when we got there the place was packed to the tree-tops with folk in their Sunday best. A record gate we had that day, as a matter of fact.

The afternoon concert went off grand, and we had a very nice boiled-ham tea, I remember, before setting about the evening programme. This was when Dave and Tommy were going to do their stuff. You know, I've been in brass banding for nigh on forty year and I've heard some stock o' cornet players in me time; but I've never enjoyed owt so much as hearing them two lads play that night. They played like angels: they were like somebody possessed. One of the pieces we did was *Alpine Echoes*, and we had Dave on the platform and Tommy up a tree in the park, echoing him. Wonderful! And the clapping! I didn't know park audiences had it in 'em. But you know, I shouldn't have liked to pick between the two lads.

Well, when we'd played *The Queen* the lads hopped it and the rest of us went across the road to The Weavers for a sneck-lifter before going home. We'd be in there about three-quarters of an hour, I should think. And when we got back to the bus who should be there but Dave and Tommy; Tommy sitting inside on his own and Dave prowling about outside, reckoning to look how the bus was put together. We all climbed in, reckoning that we thought nowt of it, though we could see from their faces that all wasn't well. And in the end we couldn't hold it any longer and we gave Short Fred the nudge, seeing as how he knew 'em best, and he asked 'em what was wrong.

Well, Dave looks down at his feet, then sneaks a glance at Tommy, who's begun to colour up a bit. Then he says, 'She's gone.' Just like that. 'She's gone.'

'Gone?' we says. 'How d'you mean, gone?'

'I mean what I say,' Dave says, a bit short like. 'She's gone with another chap.'

And then Tommy finds his voice, and he was all choked up he was so mad. 'Aye,' he says, 'I know him an' all. He's a blitherin' *accordion* player from Bradford.'

Well, we just gaped at 'em for a minute, and then somebody started to laugh, and in a second we were all at it, fit to bust. And all of us rolling about helpless seemed to bring the lads round; because in a minute Dave gives a sheepish grin and looks at Tommy, and Tommy grins back. And before we're home they're sitting together and chatting away as though they'd never heard of a lass called Cynthia.

'And that's how it's been ever since,' Sam said. 'They just got married this morning. Both of 'em. Double wedding.'

'To two girls, of course,' I said.

'Oh aye,' said Sam. 'But twins. Lasses from down in Cressley. Alike as two peas, they are. Nobody but Dave and Tommy seems to be able to tell 'em apart.'

He lifted his glass and drank. I looked up in time to catch a broad wink directed at me over the rim.

'Course, now we're all wondering what's going to happen next.'

70

Travellers

Who they were, where they had come from and where they were going, I never did find out. There were times afterwards, in memory, when they seemed unreal; though they were real enough and welcome that night as they filed into the waiting-room out of the November fog which had clamped down on the country from coast to coast, disrupting my planned journey by bus and sending me to the little out-of-the-way junction to wait for the last train to the city, fifteen miles away.

There were about twenty of them; a nondescript bunch of sober, respectable men and women of varying ages. They crowded into one end of the narrow room, surrounding and hiding the heavy bare table as they huddled in their topcoats and made wry jokes about the weather outside. One man stood out from the rest by virtue of his dress as well as his general demeanour. He seemed to be in a position of authority or responsibility towards the others: in some way their leader; and they regarded him with restrained amusement as well as respect. He had already spoken to me as they came in, making some conventional remark about the state of the night, and now I looked at him with interest.

He was a small man with a red fleshy face and pince-nez perched on his fat little nose. He wore a dove-grey homburg hat tipped back from his forehead and his navy-blue double breasted overcoat hung open to reveal a blue polka-dot bow tie and a fawn waistcoat. But what really took my eye were the felt spats which showed below the turn-ups of his grey-striped trousers. It was a

71

long time since I'd seen a man in spats. He had altogether rather an air about him; a presence and a sense of dash exemplified by his clothes and the expansiveness of his gestures, which latter were no doubt heightened by the contents of the flat half-bottle of whisky whose neck protruded from one of the pockets of his overcoat.

I'd not been alone the entire time before this invasion. One would have expected any infusion of extra human warmth to alleviate the cheerless atmosphere of that bare room, but the entry of these earlier people, ten minutes after my arrival, had seemed to lower the temperature rather than raise it.

There were three of them: a middle-aged couple and an old man, tall and lean as a garden rake, who walked between them. The younger man had answered my good evening but the woman's response was to pierce me with a gimlet look, as though she suspected me of being an exponent of the three-card trick out to fleece them of their money, or a salesman who would spend the waiting-time unloading on to them fifteen volumes of an expensive and unwanted encyclopedia.

Since then there had been no communication between us, not even the crossing of a glance. At the entrance of the little man's group they were still sitting motionless on the bench near the fireless grate, the couple like sentinels, one on each side of the old man, who seemed to be sunk in a coma, totally unaware of his surroundings, his gaze fixed on the floor some distance beyond the polished toes of his black boots. A narrow band of black material encircled the grey herring-bone tweed of his left arm. The woman was looking disapprovingly towards the crowded end of the room from behind round spectacles. I guessed she was a woman who looked disapprovingly at most things.

It had struck me a few minutes after their appearance that the group must be a choir, for they all carried bound copies of what looked like music. And as if to confirm my guess the little man now lifted his voice and addressed them all.

'We've got a while to wait, so what about a song to keep us warm?' There was a general murmur of assent followed by good-humoured groans and jeers as the little chap went on, 'Not that any chance to practise comes amiss, eh?'

He stood before them, his shoulders thrown back, regarding them with an almost comical assurance. He could handle them, I thought. He might be a slightly humorous figure but he knew how to deal with them.

'Well, sort yourselves out, then,' he said. 'Let's not get sloppy, because an audience is an audience, however small.' He half-turned and bowed his head in acknowledgement of our presence as the members of the choir reshuffled themselves and waited for his signal to begin. He pondered for a moment, then announced a piece whose name I didn't recognize, and the choir fell silent as he raised his arms.

It was as they burst into song that the old man's head lifted and turned. Something came to life in his eyes and the long fingers of each hand slowly clenched and unclenched themselves. The music was open-throated and stirring, designed to display the blend of the full choir, and the conductor guided it with flamboyant but accurate sweeps of his hands, his head cocked back and an expression of ecstasy on his plump shining face.

The old man suddenly stirred and got up, and before his companions had realized it he was striding down the room to stand at the end of the line of tenors. His head came up and his throat vibrated as he joined his voice to the singing.

The couple exchanged surprised glances and the woman said something to the man, her mouth snapping peevishly shut at the end of it. The man glanced uncertainly at the body of singers and the woman gave him a dig of the elbow which brought him to his feet. He crossed the room and took the old man's elbow and tried to lead him away. The old man was now singing at the pitch of his voice and the sound carried clear and wavering above that of the other singers. He shrugged

73

the younger man off and the other said something to him and took his arm again.

Just then the conductor noticed the little scene and called out over the choir, 'Let him alone. He's all right. Singing does you good. It's a tonic.'

This seemed to nonplus the younger man and he stood for a moment looking uncomfortable before returning to his seat. The woman gave him a furious look as he sat down, and made as if to rise herself. But he restrained her with his hand and his lips formed the words, 'Leave him alone. He's all right.'

The woman went off into a long muttered harangue during which the man looked sheepishly at the floor. Then she nudged him as though to prod him into action again as the choir came to the end of their piece and the conductor applauded vigorously, shouting, 'Bravo, bravo! Lovely, lovely,!' He took the whisky bottle out of his pocket and tilted it to his mouth.

'Now then,' he said. 'What about another one, eh. What this time? I know, I know. An old one. A real old favourite. *Love's old sweet song.*'

A moment later, before the little conductor could gather his importance round him and lift his arms, the old man had started the song in the still true, still sweet, but weak and quavering relic of what must, years before, have been a telling tenor voice:

' "Oft in the dear dead days beyond recall . . ." '

And the conductor, recovering from his momentary surprise, gazed fondly at the old man, holding back the choir until the chorus and then bringing them in, deep and sweet and rich:

' "Just a song at twilight, when the lights are low, and the flickering shadows softly come and go . . ." '

I watched and listened, my spine cold. For the old song had associations with my life, bringing memories of my mother's contralto voice and the gaiety and fun of family parties, so long ago . . .

' "Comes love's sweet song, comes lo-oves old swe-et song . . ." '

74

The music died into a hush. No-one spoke or moved for several moments. The old man stood absolutely still, staring somewhere before him. Then the woman nudged her companion again and he went over and touched the old man's arm. The old man came this time, unresisting, and as he turned fully towards me I saw that his face was livid with emotion, his eyes bright and shining in the waiting-room lights. He was two steps from his seat when it all left him in a sudden draining of life and energy that took the use from his limbs and sent him slumping to the floor. At that moment too there was the clank of the loco outside and the porter stuck his head in at the door.

'This is it. The last one tonight.'

The choir broke their ranks and moved out in a body. As the little conductor brushed by some instinct made me reach out and lightly lift the whisky bottle from his pocket. The couple had got the old man on to the bench but he hadn't come round. I went over to them.

'Come on,' I said, 'I'll help you to get him on to the train.'

With his arms round our shoulders the younger man and I carried him between us to the waiting train and struggled him into a compartment where we laid him out on the seat. The woman got in behind us, clucking with exasperation. The porter slammed the door, a whistle sounded and the train jerked into motion.

'I knew we never should have come,' the woman said. 'I knew from the start 'at it was foolish; but he would have his way. And now look at him. It might be the end of him.'

I got the whisky bottle out. 'Hold his head up,' I said to the man, who was gazing helplessly at the prostrate figure on the seat. He put his arm under the old man's head and raised it.

'He's teetotal, y'know,' the woman said, looking at the whisky. 'He never touches strong drink.'

'He's ill too,' I said. 'It won't do him any harm.'

I put the bottle to the old man's lips and let a few drops

of whisky trickle into his mouth, at the same time slipping my other hand inside his coat to feel for his heart.

'Wrap your overcoat up and put it under his head,' I said to the younger man.

The woman leaned forward from the opposite seat, the lenses of her glasses glinting in the light. 'Are you a doctor?' she said.

I said no, letting a few more drops of whisky trickle into the old man's throat. His breathing was becoming stronger.

'Will he be all right?' the man asked and I nodded. 'I think he's coming round now.'

We sat in a row and looked at the old man.

'I knew we never should have come,' the woman said again, and the man rubbed the palms of his hands nervously together between his knees.

I put the whisky away to give back to the little conductor when we got off the train. I imagined he'd be missing it by now.

'All that way,' the woman said. 'Thirty mile there and thirty mile back. And a cemetery on the doorstep! I told him, but he wouldn't listen. Stupid. Stubborn.'

'He's her father,' the man said to me. 'We've been to bury his wife. Not her mother; his second wife. She came from up Clibden. Happy you know it.'

'A little place, up on the moors, isn't it?'

'That's right. Miles from anywhere. He met her while he was out hiking one day. They used to laugh about it together and say how near he'd come to missing her. He'd reckon he wished he'd taken another turning. "I never knew what wa' waiting for me up that lane," he used to say.'

His voice sank to a confidential whisper. 'The wife, y'know, she didn't approve of the trip. She said we should've buried her nearer home, in the family grave. But he said he'd always promised to take her back there if she went first. We never thought he'd go through with it, it being winter an' all that. But we couldn't budge him. We never should've humoured him, though. The wife's right: we should've made him bury her at home. It's been too much for him. I don't suppose he'll ever be right again now ... An' all that singin' ... Whatever made him do a thing like that, d'you think? After he's been to a funeral, eh? I thought the wife 'ud die of shame when he got up like that and sang at the top of his voice.'

I looked at the old man as his son-in-law's voice droned fretfully on and thought of him in the waiting-room, singing the old songs ... 'Just a song at twilight, when the lights are low ...'

Then the woman spoke up suddenly from the other side of her husband. 'The trouble with old people,' she said, 'is they've no consideration.'

'No,' I said.

Holroyd's Last Stand

Mrs Holroyd first gets wind of it when she finds a small lace-edged handkerchief in the pocket of her husband's best suit one morning when he is down the pit. She wonders, of course, as any wife would, and realizes there could be, and no doubt is, a perfectly reasonable explanation for its presence there. He could have picked it up on the street or found it in a bus. After all, he has never given her cause to suspect him before. True, Holroyd was a ladies' man at one time, but that was years and years ago and marriage has long since cured him of the urge to wander. That and age. Or so she has always thought. For the brash cockiness of the well-built florid youth has long ago changed into the dour taciturnity of a middle-aged man who works hard in a man's world. He neglects her, of course; but how many women in the village could say otherwise? To a miner there is a man's world and a woman's, and the two make contact only at the table, in bed, and sometimes on weekend evenings in the pubs and clubs. But all the same, there is a code, and Holroyd has never carried on with other women, she is sure. At least, she always has been sure because she has never given the idea a moment's thought. But now? Who knows what he really does on his many nights out?

Mrs Holroyd leaves the handkerchief where she found it and says nothing. The morning after Holroyd has worn the suit again she looks for it and finds it gone, which makes her wonder still more and prompts her to begin examining his clothes regularly. What she hopes to find she is never quite sure but her watch is rewarded a week later when she finds in another pocket of the same suit a partly expended packet of an article she and Holroyd have never used in their married life. And then she wonders in silence no longer but calls her two married daughters to her side and divulges all.

The person concerned being their father, they are at first shocked and then, more naturally, angry.

'The old devil,' says Gladys, the elder daughter.

'After you've given him the best years of your life,' says Marjorie, who reads a great many romantic novelettes and held out for some time against the local lads, waiting for the coming of a tall, dark, pipe-smoking man with expensive tastes in fast sports cars, only to wind up married to a young collier from the next street, who smokes the cheapest fags and can afford nothing more dashing than a pedal cycle against the competition of a new baby in each of the first five years of their marriage.

'This is the thanks you get,' Marjorie goes on, 'for working your fingers to the bone for him.'

'Well, what are we going to do about it?' says Gladys, the practical one.

'Aye, you can't let him get away with it.'

Mrs Holroyd, after revealing the evidence of her husband's guilt, feels mildly inclined to his defence. 'I would like a bit more proof,' she says uncertainly.

'Proof!' Marjorie exclaims. 'What more proof do you want than them things? Ugh! Mucky things. I wouldn't have one in my house.'

'Where d'you think he meets her?' Gladys asks, and Mrs Holroyd shakes her head.

'Nay, you know as much as I do now. Sheffield, I suppose. I shouldn't think he'd do it too near home. He'd be too frightened o' being seen.'

'It'll be when he goes to t'Dogs,' Gladys says. 'Happen he doesn't go to t'Dogs at all, but meets her, whoever she is.'

'Happen he takes her to t'Dogs,' Mrs Holroyd says.

'The cheek of the old devil,' Marjorie says.

'We'll soon find out,' Gladys says with determination. 'Next time he goes I'll be on the bus before him an' waiting. I'll soon fathom his little game.'

'Suppose he sees you?' her mother says. 'An' what will you tell your Jim?'

'He won't see me,' Gladys says. 'An' I'll think of summat to tell Jim. An' not a word to Harry, Marjorie. We don't want *them* getting ideas.'

A fortnight later mother and daughters hold another conference.

'There's no doubt about it, then,' Mrs Holroyd says. 'He's carrying on.'

'The same one every time,' Gladys says.

'A fast-looking piece, I suppose?' her mother says.

'A bit simple-looking, if you ask me,' says Gladys. 'All milk an' water and a simpering smile. Just the sort to suck up to me dad an' make him think he's a big man.'

'Aye,' Mrs Holroyd says, 'he allus liked lasses sucking up to him as a lad. But I thought he'd grown out of that years ago.'

'They never grow out of it,' Gladys says.

'I wouldn't ha' classed all men alike before this,' her mother says. 'But now . . .'

'Now we know,' Marjorie says.

'Aye,' Gladys echoes, 'now we know. And we've got to decide what to do about it . . . Put the kettle on, Mother.'

'Is that a new tie you've got on?' Mrs Holroyd is asking her husband one evening a few days later.

'This? Oh, aye, aye. I saw it in a shop winder in Calderford t'other Saturday afternoon an' took a fancy to it.'

'Very smart,' Mrs Holroyd says. 'Your shoes are over here when you want 'em. I've given 'em a rub over.'

'Eh? What? Have you?' Holroyd glances at her in the mirror where he is combing his thinning black hair.

'Aye. You don't want mucky shoes when you've got a new tie on, do you?'

'No, that's right. Thanks very much.'

'I don't like to see a man become careless with his appearance as he gets older,' Mrs Holroyd says, stirring the fire with the poker. 'When a man's smart it shows he's got an interest in life.'

'Aye. I suppose you're right.'

'Dogs tonight, eh?'

'Aye, that's right – t'Dogs.'

'Does your lady friend like t'Dogs?' Mrs Holroyd asks, and Holroyd, suddenly very still, shoots her a startled look in the mirror.

'Eh?' he says. 'What's that?'

'Your lady friend,' Mrs Holroyd says. 'That young woman friend of yours in Sheffield.'

'Well, I, er . . .'

'Now don't tell me you didn't think I knew,' Mrs Holroyd says. 'Though you have kept pretty quiet about her, I must say.'

Holroyd turns from the glass and bends for his shoes, saying nothing.

'You're not ashamed of her, are you?' Mrs Holroyd asks. 'She's not deformed, is she?'

'Oh, no, no,' says Holroyd, darting perplexed looks at her now, which is easy enough to do since she doesn't once meet his eyes.

Only when he is on the point of leaving, and showing signs of wanting to get away without further conversation, does she transfix him at the door by looking him straight in the face and saying:

'Well, why don't you bring her and let's have a look at her?'

He gapes, flabbergasted. 'Bring her here?'

'Aye, why not? Bring her to tea sometime.'

He looks at her for several moments during which the frown on his face gives way to a glint in his eyes.

'All right,' he says finally, a half-embarrassed but defiant note in his voice, 'I will. I'll bring her o' Sunday.'

'Aye,' Mrs Holroyd agrees, turning away. 'Sunday. That'll be nice.'

'Come in, then,' Holroyd says. 'C'mon, don't be shy.' He takes the young woman by the arm and pulls her off the dark step and into the kitchen.

'What d'you want potterin' about at back door for?' Mrs Holroyd says. 'T'front door's for visitors. Anyway, come in, don't hang about in t'doorway.'

'Dyed hair,' is Mrs Holroyd's first thought as the young woman steps into the light.

'Well, er . . .' Holroyd says, 'this is Ella, er, Miss Fairchild. And this is my, er, Alice.'

'How d'ye do, Miss Fairchild,' says Mrs Holroyd.

'Pleased to meet you, I'm sure,' says Miss Fairchild, blinking in the strong light of the kitchen bulb. Her eyes are very blue in a doll-like face and though her features give her an appearance of youth she won't, Mrs Holroyd is sure, ever see thirty-five again.

'I've heard quite a lot about you from William,' Miss Fairchild says.

'Oh, have you now? You've told her a lot about me, have you?'

'Well, I, er . . .' Holroyd says.

'Oh, yes, he's often spoken of you. And always with the most gentlemanly respect.'

'Well, that's nice to know.' Mrs Holroyd gives a side-long glance at Holroyd, who avoids her eyes.

'Yes, I said to him once, I said, "Now see here, William, you must tell me about your wife. What sort of woman is she? I want to know all about her." '

'Oh, did you now?'

Holroyd clears his throat noisily.

'Of course, I never thought I'd meet you.'

'No, I don't suppose you did.'

'No. Not all wives would understand a relationship like mine and William's.'

'You don't think so?'

'No, you see—'

'Er, let's go into t'other room, shall we?' Holroyd says. 'Out of Alice's way.'

'Aye, you go on,' Mrs Holroyd says. 'I really can't do with you standing on top of me when I'm trying to make the tea.'

They go through into the living-room and Mrs Holroyd gets on with preparing the tea while their conversation mumbles through to her. Miss Fairchild seems to be doing most of the talking.

'Asked him all about me, did she?' Mrs Holroyd thinks. 'Wouldn't understand their relationship. Mmm. Well, well!'

Twenty minutes later Mrs Holroyd is asking their visitor how she takes her tea when the front door opens without ceremony and Gladys walks in.

'Oh,' she says, 'I didn't know you had company.'

'Come in, come in,' her mother says. 'This your father's lady friend, Miss Fairchild . . . My elder daughter, Gladys.'

Miss Fairchild says she is pleased to see Gladys and blushes. 'I'm sure I didn't think I was going to meet all the family.'

'Oh, don't mind me,' Gladys says. 'I'm allus popping in like this. I live just up the street, y'see.'

'I do think it's nice when families don't split up and drift apart,' Miss Fairchild says.

'Oh, we're big family people round here, y'know,' Gladys says. 'We stick together. Have you got no family, then?'

Miss Fairchild says with momentarily downcast eyes that she is all alone in the world, which is why she values friendship so much.

'Aye, well,' Gladys says with a laugh, 'you know what they say: you can pick your friends but you're stuck with your family. Happen you're luckier than you think.'

'Oh, I wouldn't say that,' Miss Fairchild says. 'But life has its compensations.' This with a quick fluttering glance at Holroyd, who is gazing rigidly at his plate and does not respond.

'Have a cup o' tea love?' Mrs Holroyd asks.

Gladys says she ought to be going and making Jim's tea, but she won't refuse. She takes off her coat and settles into a chair by the fire.

'You're quiet, Dad,' she says then, and Holroyd starts and says, 'Oh, aye, well . . .'

'Too many women about the place for you, is that it? Me dad was glad when me an' our Marjorie got married, y'know, Miss Fairchild. Can't stand a crowd o' women jabberin' round him.'

'Oh, I know he's a man's man,' Miss Fairchild says, casting another glance at Holroyd, who hunches a little farther down into his collar, as though to hide his head.

'You think so, do you? We've allus thought of him as a ladies' man, haven't we, mother?'

'Nay, look here . . .' Holroyd begins.

'Now you can't deny you had all the lasses on a string when you were a young feller,' Gladys says. 'I've heard 'em talk about it.'

'But that's thirty year ago.'

'There's no need to deny it for my benefit, William,' Miss Fairchild says, and Gladys suppresses a giggle into something that sounds like a sneeze.

'Have you caught a cold, Gladys?' her mother enquires.

'No, just a bit o' dust up me nose.'

'Nay, there's no dust in here. I had a right good clean down when I knew your father's friend was coming.'

'You know,' Miss Fairchild says, 'you shouldn't have gone to all that—'

'Oh, I have me pride, Miss Fairchild, even if I have been married thirty years come next Easter. I like things to be clean and tidy. Particularly on special occasions like this.'

'Eeh, you know, I wish our Marjorie 'ud pop in,' Gladys says, 'She'll be wild if she knows she's missed you. She doesn't get out all that much, y'know, with five bairns to see to. Did you know me dad was a grandfather seven times over, Miss Fairchild?'

'So many,' Miss Fairchild murmurs. 'And I dare say he's proud of them all.'

'Oh, aye, aye. My eldest is a bit too big to bounce on his knee now, but he's proud of 'em. An' they're proud of him. There isn't one of 'em 'at doesn't come running the minute they see him.'

The fire is burning low and Mrs Holroyd piles more coal on to it. Then, tea finished, they move away from the table and sit round the hearth while Gladys keeps up a cheerful monologue punctuated by remarks that she really will have to go, she only called in for a minute, and isn't it a pity that Marjorie hasn't popped in to see her father's friend. She is just saying that she'll call on her way home and tell Marjorie to come round when her sister comes into the house through the back door.

Like Gladys, Marjorie expresses surprise at the presence of 'company' and says she is only staying a minute. Like Gladys also she takes a cup of tea from the replenished pot and joins the group round the fire. Gladys changes her mind about leaving and she and Marjorie carry on a conversation occasionally added to by Mrs Holroyd, while Miss Fairchild sits with a bemused little smile on her face and looks now and again at Holroyd who is keeping quiet and still, like a man who has walked into a patch of attractive forest and suddenly wonders about the presence of wild animals.

He has not spoken for half an hour, nor even drawn attention to himself by lighting a cigarette, when Marjorie says suddenly, 'What a lovely frock you've got on, Miss Fairchild. I've been admiring it ever since I came in.'

Miss Fairchild's soft mouth purses with pleasure. 'Oh, do you really like it?'

'It shows off your figure lovely,' Gladys says. 'I reckon *he*'ll like it for that, eh?'

Miss Fairchild turns a delicate pink. 'As a matter of fact,' she says, 'he chose it.'

'O-hoh!' Gladys says, while Holroyd gives a startled glance from his eye corners. 'And paid for it, I'll bet!'

'Well' – Miss Fairchild stifles a little giggle – 'he's very generous, you know.'

'Oh, aye, he always was free with his money,' Mrs Holroyd says, adding as though in casual afterthought, 'outside the house.'

Again Holroyd seems to shrink in his chair, as though wishing to hide inside his clothes. Still he says nothing.

' 'Course, I couldn't wear a frock like that,' Marjorie says frankly. 'I'm too fat. But I bet our Gladys 'ud look well in it.'

'D'you think so?' Gladys says.

'Aye, I do.'

'I wonder, Miss Fairchild,' Gladys says eagerly, 'would you let me try it on? Such a lovely frock.'

'Well, I . . .'

'We can pop into the bedroom. It'll only take a minute.'

Miss Fairchild looks at Holroyd as though for guidance, but he is gazing fixedly into the fire and will not meet her glance. She stands up, her hands fluttering uncertainly at the waist of the frock, and Gladys and Marjorie take her out of the room and up the stairs. Now Holroyd lights a cigarette and draws on it deeply. Mrs Holroyd pours herself another cup of tea. They sit without looking at each other.

Upstairs in the front bedroom Gladys is pulling the dress down over her head and shoulders while Miss Fairchild shivers in her slip.

'Mmm,' Gladys says, turning one way then the other in front of the wardrobe mirror and smoothing the frock over her hips. 'Not bad.'

'A bit on the long side, though, isn't it?' Marjorie says, standing back and examining her sister.

'Ye-es. It'd need a couple of inches off the hem for me.'

'Well, that's easy.' Marjorie opens a drawer of the dressing-table and takes out a pair of scissors. Before the horrified eyes of its owner she bends and sticks the blades through the hem of the dress.

'Stop it!' Miss Fairchild shrieks.

She starts towards them but is abruptly stopped short

when Marjorie turns and straightens up, giving her in the same movement a slap that sends her backwards on to the bed.

Marjorie sprawls across her with her full weight, turning a corner of the eiderdown over Miss Fairchild's head to muffle her cries.

'All right. I can hold her.'

Gladys takes off the dress, slips into her own jumper and skirt, and picks up the scissors.

Holroyd turns his eyes to the ceiling. 'What's going on up there?'

'They're havin' a woman to woman talk,' his wife says. She reaches for the poker and balances it in her hand as though deciding whether or not to stir the fire.

It is the sight of Miss Fairchild as she bursts into the room uttering little shrieks of near-hysterical anger, the remnants of her dress clutched in her hands, that brings Holroyd to his feet, his mouth agape.

'What's up?' Mrs Holroyd says. 'Don't tell me you've never seen her in her underwear afore.'

'My dress,' Miss Fairchild cries. 'Oh, look what they've done to my lovely dress!'

'What you done?' Holroyd demands as his daughters come into the room. 'What you been up to?'

Miss Fairchild is sobbing noisily now as she looks at the frock. 'It's ruined,' she says, 'completely ruined.' She turns a distorted face on Holroyd. 'This would never have happened if you hadn't brought me here.'

'Get him to buy you another,' Gladys says, 'if he's gormless enough.' She has Miss Fairchild's coat now and she thrusts it into the woman's arms. 'Now hoppit!'

She and Marjorie push her through the kitchen, open the door and propel her into the darkness of the yard, and at the same time Mrs Holroyd places her hand squarely in the middle of her husband's chest and pushes him back into his chair. The girls return to the room and Holroyd cowers away as he sees the expression in the three pairs of eyes levelled at him.

'Now for you,' Marjorie says.

Five minutes later, kicked, scratched and bruised, he is on his hands and knees in the backyard. The door slams behind him and the bolt shoots home.

There is no sign of Miss Fairchild. Holroyd himself does not come home for three days. But Mrs Holroyd does not mind. She spends a very interesting time discussing with her daughters new ways of making his life miserable when he does return.

A Casual Acquaintance

I was twenty that autumn. It was quite simple the way it happened. I noticed her for the first time on the bus on the journey home from the office one Friday afternoon and fell in love with her on the spot. I pointed her out with studied casualness to my friends Larry and Peter, but neither of them knew her.

I thought about her all weekend and looked out for her every afternoon of the following week. But it wasn't until Friday that I saw her again; for although this was the only afternoon my office closed at five, she evidently travelled at the same time every day. So I watched for her on the one day only and a Friday without my seeing her left me downcast for days, my spirits rising only when the weekend was well behind and another Friday approaching fast.

For weeks I was content just to look at her: to get on to the bus, my heart racing with excitement at the possibility of seeing her and, if it was a lucky Friday, taking a seat from which I could observe without being noticed and gazing at her all the way into town. In the bus station, where we both alighted, I'd stand and watch her cross to her connection, small, straightbacked, with a poise that singled her out from her contemporaries, and a slight haughtiness in the set of her head and the cool glance of brown eyes in a heart-shaped face that chilled in me any notion of a brash approach, a high-handed sweeping aside of the formalities that stood between us.

One Friday afternoon she was talking to another girl as I boarded the bus and brushed past her. I heard her addressed as Joyce. It excited me to have a name by which to think of her. It identified her and made me determined to find out still more about her.

That same afternoon I followed her across the bus station and got on to the same bus. It took us out to the other side of town. An acute fear of appearing conspicuous stopped me from following her to her door, but I watched where she alighted, and at the next stop I jumped off myself and caught a bus back into town. Now I knew her first name and roughly where she lived, and as I rode home I thought that with this increase in my knowledge of her the time was surely approaching when we should meet and really know each other. As it was now, I thought with sudden gloom, she was probably not even aware of my existence, let alone my feeling for her.

As the weeks passed by with no progress made I began, on the evenings when I could leave my studies, to take long walks into the district where she lived. I'd get off the bus and stroll up the road which wound away over the hill and into the next valley. On the brow of the hill I'd stop for a while, leaning on the wall and looking out over the dark forest of chimneys at the lights of the town.

Away in the distance, on my left, I could see the lighted windows of a huge mill working the night shift. It seemed to me like a great ship floating on a sea of night; full of souls, hundreds of people, whom I would never see and never know. I thought then of the wonderful chance that had singled Joyce out for me; and it seemed to me in some way preordained that that same chance would eventually bring us together. I was sure of it.

From the top of the hill I wandered back through side-streets and looked at the curtained windows of strange houses and wondered if she was inside, living her life. On all these rambles through the lamplit streets, which though strange at first soon became familiar to me, I cherished vague dreams of suddenly coming face to face with her and having the right words to say. But I didn't see her once. I went on, living in a kind of suspense, loving her from a distance, waiting for the miracle that would bring us together. Until Christmas was only a fort-night away. And then it happened.

On that Saturday, two weeks before Christmas, I was in town, pressing through the throngs of shoppers to choose presents for my family. I was looking at socks in a depart-ment store when she turned her head and showed me her dear face, three counters away. I forgot my own errands at once and made my way towards her. I had no idea of accosting her but as she moved on, absorbed in her own shopping, I followed behind. She was by herself.

I kept her in sight all round the store until, at last, with her shopping bag and basket both filled, she made for the door. Alarmed then at the thought of losing her on the busy street, I pushed forward until I was immediately behind her.

I was so close I could have reached out and touched her at the moment the handle of her bag broke and half the contents spilled out on to the floor. She gave an exclama-tion of annoyance, and before I realized it I was down on my hands and knees picking up packages and putting them back in the bag.

'There.' We looked at each other as I straightened up, and I was chilled by the lack of recognition in her eyes and in a curious way astounded that she couldn't tell simply by looking at me that I'd been yearning for her all those months.

She thanked me and held out her hand for the bag, which I was holding under my arm.

'Please let me carry it for you.' I motioned to her basket. 'You can't manage them both; this handle's useless now.'

'It's very kind of you.' Her voice was doubtful, and I said, 'I can see you don't know me. But I know you. I've seen you nearly every Friday on the bus into town.'

Was it politeness or a genuine glimmer of recognition in her eyes now, as she said. 'I thought there was some-thing familiar about your face.'

It was enough for me for the moment. We moved by

common consent out of the store and on to the teeming pavement. There I looked at her. 'Which way?' I asked, and she smiled at my persistence.

'I've finished my shopping, so if you wouldn't mind walking to the bus station . . .'

'I was going that way myself,' I lied.

'I'm not taking you out of your way, then.' She gave me another of those smiles which seemed to turn my heart right over. 'But it really is very good of you.'

We walked along in comparative silence. I had the reputation among my friends of being something of a wit; but now I was almost tongue-tied and could think of only the most commonplace remarks. And soon we'd be in the bus station and it would all be over.

'This is really lucky for me,' I said all at once.

She glanced up at me. 'Oh?'

'Yes. I've seen you quite a lot these past few months and I've wanted an excuse to speak to you.'

'Oh?' she said again.

'I couldn't simply walk up to you and start talking, could I? You know with some girls you could, but not you.'

We had stopped on a corner now and she was gazing at me with hazel eyes full of bland sophistication that made me feel fourteen years old. I felt that I was on the verge of a blush; but I was determined to see it through. I might never have another chance. She glanced at her watch and I blurted out, 'Well, you see, the idea was that I should ask you to come out with me some evening.'

'But I don't know you,' she said.

'That's the trouble,' I said, feeling smaller and more foolish with every second she went on gazing up at me. 'But how else can we get to know each other?'

'No,' she said, freeing me from her direct gaze at last. 'I see your point. But I'm afraid I couldn't. My boy friend wouldn't like it, you see.'

'Oh! Your boy friend.' What a fool I was! Seeing her always alone, I'd never considered the most obvious point – that someone else might have a prior claim on her.

She went on, blasting all my hopes and driving me

deeper into confusion. 'He doesn't live round here and we only see each other at weekends; but he wouldn't like me to go out with anybody else during the week.'

'No,' I babbled. 'No, of course not.' All I could think of now was what a fool I must look to her. I gave her back her shopping bag. 'I'm sorry I said anything.'

Going home, I thought that these things worked only in books or on the films; in real life you were just made to look silly. And it was pride that was really uppermost in my mind now. So long as she didn't turn the incident into a joke to tell to her friends, it mightn't be too bad. I'd told nobody about her; not even Larry and Peter; and I was even less inclined to take them into my confidence now.

But when that confusion had left me I realized that the setback had not changed my feelings about her. I abandoned my evening walks but still watched for her on Friday afternoons. And now the ice was broken; we could greet each other as acquaintances, and she did at least acknowledge my existence by letting me ride with her into town and talking with me while we waited for our connections. Sometimes Peter, who lived out in my direction, would be with us, but more often we were alone. All the rest of the winter my mind was full of her, and the idea that, if only I were patient, she might one day turn to me became the great impossible dream of my life. My feeling for her deepened steadily, strengthened by the very absence of encouragement, until it seemed to me that all the wonder and delight of Woman was contained in her sweet and gentle self. And, sustained by my dream, I went on wooing her passively by my presence on those short homeward journeys on the one afternoon in the week.

On an afternoon in March, with the days lengthening into spring, we stood together chatting idly in the bus station. I was talking about a film I'd seen at the weekend. She mentioned then that she'd spent the weekend indoors and, wondering at this, I mentioned my unknown rival for the first time.

'He's neglected you for once, then?' I said, trying to keep my voice light.

'For always,' she said. 'It's over. It has been for weeks.'

My heart gave a tremendous leap of joy. Over! Then there was nothing to stop her going out with me.

'Are you still thinking about that?'

'Of course.' Oh, God, wasn't it all I'd been able to think about since I first saw her!

'But why?' she said, and it seemed to me that there was a great weariness in her voice. 'We're friends, aren't we? Isn't that enough for you?'

'It can never be enough.'

'But why?' she said again.

'Because . . . because I like you too much.' No, it wasn't good enough. I had to say it, even here in broad daylight, among streams of people. I must say it. 'Because I love you.'

She shook her head. 'It's no use. I'm sorry, Clive, but it could only lead to disappointment. People never live up to expectation, you know.'

It needed only one word from her to make my world a place of life and joy and laughter; and I was shocked by the disillusionment in her voice. 'Why..that's defeatism! Look, maybe you are a bit cut up just now, but you can't look at life in general like that.'

'It's the way things are,' she said with quiet finality. 'It's the way it goes.'

I could only think she had loved him very much, and envy him for that. Whatever had happened between them had hurt her badly. Frantically, I searched for something else to say, then gave it up as I realized that it was no good. I knew with miserable certainty that it never had been.

I saw her several times more before summer came, bringing with it the end of my deferment and a summons to serve a postponed period of National Service.

I took a job in Wales when I came out of the army and it was only on infrequent weekends that I went home to

94

see my family. As time went by I lost touch with Larry and Peter and I saw neither of them for several years until I ran into Larry quite accidentally while on a visit home. It was lunchtime and we went into a pub to talk over a glass of beer. Larry had been working away too – in London – but he'd married now and returned to settle in his home town.

'And Peter,' I said when we'd gossiped for a while. 'What's he doing nowadays?'

'He's in the Merchant Navy. Third Engineer. Or is it Fourth? I forget now.'

'I seem to remember hearing he'd got married too.'

'Lord, yes!' Larry's ugly mobile face screwed itself into a grimace of disgust. 'Bought himself a real packet there. He signed on to get away from it all.'

'As bad as that, eh? Who did he marry? A local girl?'

'Called Joyce Henryson. Used to work up the road from us. That's how he met her. On the bus.'

'Joyce Henryson?' Could it be? I tried to analyse the feeling the name evoked in me. How long since she'd been in my thoughts? I could almost feel myself blushing now at my past folly. But trouble?

'That's right,' Larry said. 'You knew her. You used to ride down into town with her, didn't you? I remember thinking at one time that you'd a fancy for her yourself.'

'And you say old Peter went to sea to get away from her?'

'He certainly did, mate. What a so-and-so she turned out to be! He always knew she liked a good time, mind. He was mad about her, but after they were married he just couldn't keep up with her. He wrote to me and I got him a job with my firm in London. The money was better but she wouldn't move and he was no better off, trying to keep both ends going and seeing her only once every few weeks.'

I drank from my glass, listening to him.

'A sorry tale, Clive. Then . . . well, he eventually found out that she was carrying on with a bloke she'd known years back. A married man. Seemed she'd had an unhappy affair with him then, and now he'd left his wife and there was nothing standing between them but poor old Peter. She seemed to blame him for that. I tell you, she got him so he didn't know what he was doing. And you know what a steady lad he always was.'

I nodded. 'It'll be divorce, then?'

'The sooner he gets rid, the better.'

We drank in silence for some minutes.

'No signs of you getting hitched, then, Clive?'

'No . . . I haven't found the right one, I suppose.'

'Yes, it's fine if you get the right one; and hell if you pick a wrong 'un.'

'You know,' I said in a moment, 'she never struck me as being that sort.'

'Nor Peter, evidently. Still, you never did know her well, did you?'

I looked at the amber dregs of my beer. Of course I was thinking – would it have been different with me? Could I have held her or would I have got the same rotten deal as Peter? And how rotten did the deal seem to her? They were things I'd never know.

'No,' I said at length. 'No, she was just a casual acquaintance.'

Waiting

Old Thompson was seventy-four the winter his wife died. She was sixty-nine. They would have celebrated their golden wedding the following summer and they were a quiet and devoted couple. It was bronchitis that finished her, helped along by a week of November fog poisoned by Cressley's industrial soot and smoke. In ten days she was gone.

His wife's death nearly finished Thompson too. He was a changed man. Always active and vigorous, carrying his years lightly, and with a flush of ruddy good health in his face, he now seemed to age overnight. He seemed to shrivel and bend like a tree from whose roots all nutrition had been drained. His hands were all at once uncertain and fumbling, where they had grasped surely. The world about him seemed to lose interest for him. He became silent and withdrawn. He would sit for long hours in his tall wooden-backed armchair by the fire, and what he thought about in his silence no-one knew.

Bob, the Thompsons' younger son, and his wife Annie were living in the house in Dover Street when Mrs Thompson died. The Thompsons had had four children. The elder son was lost at sea during the war; a daughter married and emigrated to Australia, and a second daughter, Maud, fifteen years older than Bob, lived with her family in another part of the town.

Bob and Annie had not known each other long before they became eager to get married: Bob because he wanted Annie and she (though she was fond of Bob in her own way) because she could at last visualize a life away from her roughneck family. When Mrs Thompson suggested that they marry and live with them in Dover Street until they could get a house of their own, Annie hesitated. Her ideal of marriage had been a process whereby she acquired a husband and an orderly, well-furnished home in one fell swoop. But she soon saw the advantages in this arrangement. She would, first of all, escape from her present life into a house which was quiet and efficiently run, if not her own; and she would be able to go on working so that she and Bob could save up all the more quickly for their own house. She would also get Bob, a good enough husband for any working-class girl: good-natured and pliable, ready to be bent her way whenever it was necessary for her ends.

In time Bob became used to the silent figure in the house: but Annie, who since her mother-in-law's death had given up her job and was at home all day, began to find the old man's constant presence a source of growing irritation.

'He gets on me nerves, Bob,' she said one night when they were alone. 'Just sitting there all day and me having to clean up round him. And he hardly says a word from getting up in a morning to going to bed.'

'Well, I reckon he's a right to do as he likes,' Bob said mildly. 'It's his house, not ours. We're the lodgers, if anybody.'

But to Annie, now looking after the house as if it were her own, it was beginning to seem the other way about.

On Wednesday afternoons Annie took the bus into Cressley to shop in the market. For an hour or so she would traverse the cobbled alleyways between the stalls, looking at everything, buying here and there, and keeping a sharp lookout for the bargains that were sometimes to be had. And then, with all her purchases made, she would leave the market for the streets of the town to spend another hour in her favourite pastime: looking in furniture-shop windows. There were furniture shops of all kinds in Cressley, from those where you

98

had to strain your neck to see the prices on the tickets to others where you could hardly see the furniture itself for the clutter of placards and notices offering goods at prices almost too tempting to be true.

One Wednesday she found a new shop full of the most delightful things, with a notice inviting anyone to walk in and look round without obligation. Annie hesitated for a moment before stepping through the doorway where, almost at once, she stopped entranced before a three-piece suite in green uncut moquette. There was a card on the sofa which said: 'This fine 3-piece suite is yours for only ten shillings a week,' and very small at the bottom, 'Cash price eighty-nine guineas.' Ten shillings a week . . . Why, she could almost pay that out of her housekeeping and never miss it!

A voice at her shoulder startled her. 'Can I help you, Madam?' She looked round at the assistant who had come softly to her side.

'Oh, well, no,' she said, flustered. 'I was just looking.'

'Was it lounge furniture you were particularly interested in?' asked the young man.

'Well, no . . . All of it, really.'

'I see. You're thinking of setting up house?'

'Well, yes, as a matter of fact, I am. I'm just looking round, y'know, seeing what there—'

'We can supply everything you need.' The assistant took her by the elbow. 'If you'll just come up to the showroom you'll see what I mean . . .'

'Well, I . . .' Annie began, panicking a little at the thought of getting involved; but she was already being led to the rear of the shop and up a few wide steps.

In the entrance to the showroom she stopped and gaped. There before her, filling every corner of the vast room, was furniture of all shapes, sizes and uses; lounge furniture, dining-room furniture, furniture for bedroom and kitchen, and even television and wireless sets.

'You know we can furnish a complete home for only a few pounds a week . . .'

Half an hour later Annie was on the bus, going home, with pictures of beautiful rooms floating through her intoxicated mind. All that, and for just a few pounds a week. Why, there was no reason why they couldn't have their home tomorrow. No reason except they hadn't got a house.

'Bob, when are we going to have a house of our own? We've been hanging about for three years now and we're no nearer than when we got married.'

'Oh, I don't know,' Bob said easily. 'There's not a lot o' point in trying to get another place with things as they are. Besides, who'd look after me dad?'

'Your Maud might think about doing her share.'

'Aye, aye, I know,' Bob mumbled. 'Happen she'd buckle to if it came to it. She's not a bad sort at bottom, our Maud. But anyway, it hasn't come to that. Where would we go if we did move? You can't get a house to rent any more than you could three year ago.'

'What about buying one, then?' Annie said.

'We'd better wait till we've enough brass for a good deposit.'

'We've over three hundred pounds in the bank,' Annie said. 'What did we save it for?'

'You could spend all that on furniture. That wouldn't go far.'

They were walking home from the cinema after seeing a film set partly in an American house with an open split-level living-room where there was lots of space and all the furnishings looked smart and well made. Annie knew the limitations of her life and did not yearn for the impossible; but she was becoming avid now to reach out and take what was there awaiting her grasp.

'There's always hire purchase. I was talking to a feller in a shop today and he told me you could furnish a house for just a few pounds a week.'

Bob laughed. 'Had one o' them chaps on to you, have you? They'll tell you owt. No, we can do wi' out debts like that. Someday you'll have all you want.'

'Someday . . .' Annie muttered. 'Stopping at home after

100

working all that time has got me wanting a place of me own.'

'Well, I mean this place is as good as yours, isn't it? You do pretty well as you like in it, don't you? And it'll really be yours one o' these days. After all, me dad can't last—' He stopped.

Annie glanced quickly at him. 'You mean he can't last for ever.'

'Shurrup,' Bob muttered. 'We shouldn't be talking like that.'

There was a light on in the house and they found Bob's father sitting in his chair by the fire.

'Still up?' Annie said. 'I thought you'd have been in bed long since.'

The old man lifted his face to them, though his eyes seemed hardly to take them in. 'I wa' just going.'

He pulled himself up and went out without another word.

They went on as they were for some time. And then summer came and with the warmer days old Thompson stirred from his chair and began in the afternoons to stroll down the hill to the park where he could sit on a bench in the sun.

It was a great relief for Annie to be without him for a while each day, and she found new zest for her life as a housewife, the life she had always craved for from being a girl in a rough, overcrowded home. She tackled the work with great spirit, scrubbing and polishing until the house was always faultlessly clean.

But still there was something lacking. It wasn't like caring for her own possessions, for she was surrounded by furniture that was heavy and dark and old-fashioned and which never gave her a true reward for all the effort she applied to its care.

'This old furniture gives me the willies,' she complained to Bob. 'It's like living in a museum. All them chinks and crannies just harbour dust. I don't know how your mother put up with it all them years.'

'She was used to it. It's the furniture they got when they were married. It was all the fashion at one time.'

'It's out o' fashion now, all right,' Annie said.

'Aye, well, we'll have some good stuff when we get a place of our own.'

'Look, Bob,' she said, 'why don't we get some new furniture now? Think how nice this place could look with a new carpet and a three-piece suite, and—'

'Hold on a minute,' Bob said. 'What about me dad? This is his house, y'know, and he might like it as it is.'

'You can ask him. I don't think he'd mind. You know how he is these days.'

'But what could we do with his stuff?'

'Oh, we could sell it. Somebody on the market 'ud take it off our hands.'

'We can't just sell the old feller's home up round him,' Bob said. He sounded shocked at the thought. 'Dammit, what would he do when we left?'

'I don't know as there'd be any need for us to leave if we had some decent furniture,' Annie said.

Bob saw her smooth round face set stubbornly in the expression which always frightened him a little. He was still surprised she had ever married him and anxious to please her in any way he could.

'I suppose – that's to say, if me dad doesn't mind – I suppose we could put it into store. Then if he ever needed it it'd be there.'

In the event they sold the furniture, the old man offering no objection. They gave him the money, a pitifully small number of notes which he gazed at in silence for some time before closing his hand round them and putting them away.

They redecorated the living-room, using a light modern paper which seemed to push the walls back, and hung new curtains. Then when the furniture came – the carpet, the dining-suite and the three-piece – the transformation was complete and startling. Annie was ready to hug herself. Here was something worth looking after, that rewarded dusting and polishing, something that was her own. The only jarring note was struck by the old man's tall-backed chair, empty more often now in the long warm afternoons when he was sitting on a bench in the park.

For a time she was at peace. And then she could not help speaking to Bob about an unfairness that had rankled before but which seemed more obviously unjust now that the house had her own stamp on it at last. She suggested that Bob's sister be approached with a view to her taking the old man.

'We've had him for nearly a year now,' she pointed out. 'I don't see why your Maud shouldn't take her turn. She's got as much room as we have.'

'But this is his home,' Bob said. 'He won't want to go.'

'What's the difference between one place and another?' Annie said. 'He hardly knows where he is anyway.'

'I dunno,' Bob said. 'There's summat not—'

'Look, just promise you'll see her and mention it.'

'Well . . . I don't suppose there's any harm in sounding her out.'

He came into the house a few nights later to find Annie and the old man sitting on opposite sides of the hearth, his father with his hands resting on the stick between his legs as usual, but perched on the edge of one of the new armchairs. Bob looked round.

'Where's your chair, then, Dad?'

The old man's voice was stronger than he'd heard it for a long time now. 'Ask her,' he said.

Annie was blushing a fiery red. 'I . . . I let it go this afternoon,' she said. 'I sold it to a chap at the door for five bob. Your dad won't take the money.'

'You did what?' Bob said incredulously.

Annie was obviously regretting her impulse, but it was too late now.

'It was out of place here . . . And I knew your Maud wouldn't want it.'

Taken off balance as he was, Bob spoke without thinking of the old man sitting there.

103

'It's not the only thing our Maud doesn't want.'

No-one spoke for several moments and in the silence a quiver ran through old Thompson's body. He got to his feet, drawing himself erect as he faced the two of them.

'You've been round there, haven't you? Trying to get rid o' me.' His voice, pitched high and thin, cracked with his anger. 'I know what it is. You're wantin' me to die. Well, I'll tell you – I'm wantin' it an' all. There's nowt left for me sin' my Mary went. I'm waitin', just bidin' my time till the good Lord sees fit to take me to her again.' His stick rose and fell with a mighty crack against the skirting board. 'And you'll just have to bide your time an' wait anent me.'

He turned his flushed face and glittering eyes from them and went through the door. They heard his slow feet on the stairs. Neither of them spoke. In a moment they looked at each other and then they looked away.

Madge

If there was one thing all who knew Madge Collins were agreed upon it was that she was a lady: she had grace, charm, poise. Most people acknowledged her qualities with approval; in some, conscious of being lesser mortals, they aroused feelings of rancour. She was too perfect for this life, and pride went before a fall.

It had always been so with her. As a child she was a 'little madam', wilful, used to getting her own way, but without the passions, tears and sulks others found inseparable from the attaining of their ends. At twenty-nine, the eldest of the three Greenaway girls, she was still single. Her youngest sister, Angela, had got herself pregnant while still at university and married with unfortunate haste at nineteen. You couldn't imagine Madge Greenaway in a situation like that; and it was less the moral aspect of it that one saw as sitting incongruously on her personality than the simple untidiness of it; the mess. At twenty-nine she seemed to be placidly biding her time (and leaving it a touch late, some thought). Though her name had never been closely connected with any man's, no-one doubted that she'd had her chances. She was handsome, intelligent, and she would have money from her father. Potential suitors came and went. One came and stayed long enough to transfer his attentions to the middle sister, Catherine, and marry her. Nor was there any feeling in this that Madge had lost a husband, that Catherine had stolen a man from her. She was hardly aware that her future brother-in-law had come to woo her before all the attractions he thought he'd found in her were more piquantly displayed to him in the person of Catherine. Madge, who hadn't wanted him anyway, gave them her blessing and went on living her own well-ordered life. 'The man isn't born who's good enough for Madge Greenaway,' said an observant, concerned, and somewhat irritated friend at this time.

Edgar Collins changed this notion. It had been said that Madge did not meet enough eligible men because she had never gone out to work. Adam Greenaway became a widower while Madge was in her last year at school. She showed no interest in continuing her education and, at eighteen, she chose to stay at home and keep house for her father and younger sisters. Adam Greenaway was the managing director of a family motor sales and repair firm which he ran with a brother and a nephew, and there was plenty of money to pay for help for Madge. A woman came to the house every day and relieved her of all the menial tasks, leaving her free to supervise the shopping and household expenditure and to cook, all of which she enjoyed doing and showed an aptitude for. When her father, who for several years had been a Conservative member of the town council, came to serve his term as mayor, Madge became his mayoress and discharged her duties with such grace and ease she might have trained for the purpose all her life. On the occasions when she spoke in public she did so in a manner which, while not controversial, was lucid and piquant and avoided the shabby clichés so many of her predecessors had relied upon. Madge Greenaway didn't flap easily; not even when the chairman at one of the functions she opened became himself so controversial as to describe her as the most charming mayoress the town had had for many a year to an audience containing two recent holders of the office. One of them who had already despised the other for owning all the faults Madge Greenaway was so free of now found that she detested Madge Greenaway more. The second woman was honestly pleased to see someone function so admirably in a role she herself had feared and fumbled in, to the extent of tripping on the stairs at the mayor's ball and sending sprawling the first citizen of a neighbouring town. It was at the mayor's ball held during her father's year of office that Madge met Edgar Collins.

He was introduced to her across an arbitrarily come-together circle in the bar, a shortish, stocky, sandy-haired man whom she smiled at and took no more notice of until a few moments later when, Tommy Marshall having launched into a risqué story he'd been awaiting an audience for all evening, she felt a touch on her elbow and realized that Collins had edged his way round the outside of the group and was asking her to dance.

'Or would you like another drink?'

'Thank you. I think I'd prefer to dance.'

He had green eyes. His colouring wasn't of a type she had thought she cared for. She handed him her empty glass and he got rid of it before they walked together along the passage to the ballroom.

'I hope you didn't mind, but I thought a rescue operation might be in order.'

'He can be very funny at times.'

'It didn't strike me as being one of those times.'

'Perhaps you're right.'

'The dignity of the office, and all that,' he said.

'Even if the holder doesn't care . . .'

'Ah, now, I didn't say that. I was thinking about the dignity of your sex as much as anything.'

'Thank you.' She was amused.

'And somehow I turn out to sound pompous and stuffy.'

'No, I wouldn't say that.'

'I'm neither, really. And as a matter of fact, it is a very funny story.'

'Then why take me away?'

'There's a time and place for everything. If you like, I'll tell it you myself, when we get to know each other better.'

She said, lying, 'I'm sorry. I didn't catch your name.'

Collins was an architect who had a junior partnership with the ageing head of a firm in a nearby town. Some work for the Corporation had given him his connection with the Town Hall, hence his invitation to the mayor's ball where he met Madge.

He telephoned her three days later to say that he had to run out on Saturday afternoon to take a quick look at a site in Harrogate and would she like to go with him and then spend the evening in Leeds, where they could have an early dinner and go to see the touring production of a West End musical, for which he had tickets. It was the odd make-up of the invitation that stopped her from putting him off till another time. Why had he not suggested just dinner and the theatre? Why should she go all the way out to Harrogate with him?

But she went, and sat with cold feet and a mounting irritation as the warmth drained out of the stationary car and Collins and his client tramped about, pointing and talking interminably in the rapidly fading light. She tried not to show her impatience as Collins finally shook hands and came back to the car. He was himself in a mild temper.

'Idiot,' he muttered as he slammed the door and pressed the starter.

'What's the matter?'

'Oh, I'd hoped to have a quick look at the site without seeing him; but he turned up and I was forced to listen to his cockeyed ideas.'

'I thought the man who paid the piper called the tune.'

Collins grunted. 'That, if I may say so, is a typical client's attitude. He's got a nice sloping site there, with a view. He wants his sitting-room to both overlook the view *and* catch the afternoon sunlight. Unfortunately, I can't give him that without rearranging the order of the sun's coming up and going down.'

'What will you do?'

'We'll talk about it and promote a bit more bad feeling on both sides, then settle for the inevitable compromise.'

He glanced at her as he took the car round a big island on to the Leeds road. 'I'm sorry. I didn't intend to keep you hanging about for so long.'

She looked out at the coloured lights in the trees. 'I was wondering why you'd brought me out here with you.'

'I knew I shouldn't have time to go all the way back to pick you up.'

'Couldn't we have met in Leeds?'

'That would have meant you making your own way there.'

'I'm quite capable of doing that.'

'Yes, you'd either come in by bus, or in your own car. The first method is inconvenient and the second would have meant an incomplete evening: parting in Leeds instead of my driving you home.' He flicked on his headlights as they left the street-lamps on the edge of the town. 'Now I've spoiled the beginning of it by leaving you bored and cold.'

The warmth from the heater began to move round her calves and feet as they drove down the hill. Headlights swung and lifted in the sudden intense darkness as ascending cars overtook a slow-moving bus.

She said, 'All right. I'll forgive you.'

He was a logical man, who organized his life. She must overlook the small occasions when circumstances upset his plans. She leaned forward as far as the safety belt he'd insisted she wear would permit and gently rubbed her legs below her knees. He glanced at what she was doing and asked, 'Feeling warmer now?'

'Yes.' Now, she found, she was pleasantly expectant about the evening ahead.

He parked in a street off Briggate and led her round the corner to a pub in a narrow yard which was reached through an alley between two shops.

'Is this where we're going to eat?'

It wasn't what she had expected. She looked at the late-Victorian interior as they stepped inside: a low ceiling, black wood, brass rails, grey mirrors – some carrying chipped and faded advertisements for products forgotten since the First World War – and caught a glimpse past the heads of the standing drinkers of joints of roast beef and ham on a marble-topped counter. She thought, 'Oh, no, not a cold sandwich in this crush!' before feeling Collins' hand on her arm as he made way for her to follow him through to the restaurant area beyond the bar.

He gave the waitress his name and she pulled out a table so that they could sit side by side with their backs to the wall.

'Are you hungry?'

'Famished.'

'The steak and kidney pie's good. So's the fillet steak, for that matter. And to start with I can recommend either the paté or the whitebait. They're both delicious.'

They ordered, and Madge sat forward to lean on her elbows and scrutinize her surroundings from this new vantage point.

'This is a quaint place.'

'You've never been before?'

'I didn't even know it existed.'

'It can't have changed much since the turn of the century. A real old music-hall pub. Can't you imagine it full of gents with mutton-chop whiskers and ladies of doubtful reputation with low necklines, too much make-up, and big hats?'

Their drinks came. Collins lifted his glass and turned his head to look into her face. 'Cheers!'

Madge echoed him. She had speculated earlier about where he would take her if he wanted to impress her on this first evening out. The Metropole? The French restaurant at the Queen's? But she saw now that he was not the man to establish false precedents. He might indeed take her to such places sometimes, but she would know now that it was a special occasion. Impress her? She was just a little irked to realize that he had succeeded in doing that simply by not at all trying to do so.

*

110

Had her father lost his wealth Madge Greenaway would have missed what it bought, but – providing there were no attendant disgrace – she would have coped with her changed circumstances. For Madge's life was conditioned not by considerations like happiness and fulfilment, but by a sense of the fitting, and it was a sense she would have applied in whatever drawer of the social cupboard she had found herself. Not that she thought much about this. It was in instinct for the way she wished to appear to other people; and it had more to do with respect – hers for herself as she felt it reflected in the eyes of others – than with anything as obvious as popularity and being liked.

When it became clear, as it soon did, that Edgar Collins was more than casually interested in her, she began to think about the matter of marriage to him.

She wasn't in love with Collins but she was fond of him. As the junior partner in a small firm of architects he wasn't the most obviously desirable match; but he was young enough and ambitious enough to better himself, and Madge was not averse to pushing him where it might seem needed. She was nearly thirty. Opportunities for marriage were bound to become fewer. Spinsterhood, however proud, had no place in her scheme of things. She *ought* to be married.

She made up her mind; not so much that she would say yes when he asked her to marry him, but that she would lead him into a position where he would ask. For she sensed that behind the smiles, the jokes, the cool banter, Collins was a little in awe of her. Perhaps it was the enormous respect many men had for the woman with whom they were newly in love; or maybe it was simply the strength of her personality which kept him at a distance. She thought that she was, anyway, the stronger of the two; that she would lead the way here as she would, no doubt, on so many occasions in the future.

She began to charge their meetings with small intimacies: borrowing a handkerchief which she returned washed and ironed; giving him cigarettes from her own

111

lips while he was driving; letting him turn when others were there to find her watching him; and gazing at his mouth while they were alone and he was talking, in a manner that suggested a preoccupation less with what he was saying than with him himself. She wanted him to try to make love to her, to put himself into a situation over which she had full control. She didn't doubt her ability to control it. But something held him back. He took her hand in a cinema and kissed her briefly when they parted, but that was all. Collins would come to the moment in his own time, she was sure, and patience was a quality which, in maturity, she had never lacked. But there was satisfaction in controlling the pace and pattern of events, and pleasure in the thought that she might engineer the time and place herself.

But not foolishly. She went to see her doctor. He was an elderly man who had known Madge all her life.

'I know I can't expect you to approve,' she said. 'And the best precaution of all is to say no.' She was appealing in her apparent frankness. 'But you see, I can't guarantee to do that.'

He waved his hand. 'The fact that you're sensible about it is something.' He paused. 'You are a virgin?'

'Yes.'

'You've played tennis, ridden a little, led an active life . . . You should be all right in that respect. As to the other matter, I'm afraid there's not much I can suggest.' He coughed. 'At this stage, it should be up to him.'

'But I can't broach the subject till it happens. And if he hasn't—'

'Do you know anything about the so-called safe periods?'

'A little.'

'All I can say is rely on that until you can discuss the other ways with him.'

'But how do I know it will happen during . . . ?' Madge stopped. She knew he'd seen through her. She didn't care. It was her business.

'It's a risk, though, isn't it?' she said.

He swung round in his swivel chair and looked directly at her.

'I take it you intend to marry the young man?'

'Oh, yes. When he asks me.'

It happened some weeks later, when Adam Greenaway was absent on business and Madge had the house to herself. They came back from a cinema and sat drinking gin and tonic on the sofa in front of the fire. They held hands and Collins kissed her. Before long, he put aside his glass, took Madge's from her, and pushed her back into the cushions.

In a few moments Madge said firmly, 'No!'

Collins drew away at once. 'What's wrong?'

'This sordid fumbling. It's like kids with mum and dad in the other room.' She got up and stood by the fire. 'Do you seriously want me, Edgar?'

'I've wanted you for ages.'

She turned and looked at him levelly before speaking again.

'Will you give me five minutes and then come up? It's the door facing the stairs, at the end of the corridor.'

She went quickly up to her room and took off her clothes. She stood then before the full-length glass in the wardrobe door and looked at herself. Her body was one she need not be ashamed of. She wondered if she should let Collins see it now. But that, she thought, was altogether too brazen. She shivered and, turning back the sheets, got into bed, leaving only the bedside light.

Collins tapped on the door before coming in. She did not look at him and he said nothing. The rustle of his undressing was followed by a long pause because she felt his weight on the bed. Then he slid down beside her and switched off the light. He felt for her in the darkness, his hands soft and light in their touch. 'Oh, Madge, Madge, you're so very beautiful.' His breath on her face smelled of pipe tobacco and gin.

'Am I?'

His mouth felt for her breasts. It was a gamble for her. It could go wrong now in the worst possible way, make

113

her a conquest, available again. It wasn't comfortable, either. There must be more to it than this. She stiffened under him and caught her breath.

'I'm hurting you.'

'No, it's all right. It's just that I've never . . .'

'Never?' Collins asked.

She shook her head against the pillow. 'No.'

'Darling Madge. I love you.'

'Oh, do you, Edgar?'

'Madge . . . will you marry me?'

Her mouth curved as she smiled in the darkness.

'Yes, Edgar. Oh, yes.'

Some time later she felt the shaking of his body beside her.

'Edgar . . . what's the matter?'

He was laughing!

'Oh, God,' he said at last. 'I was beginning to think I'd never find the nerve to ask you.'

They were married in the parish church. Edgar Collins' parents and other members of his family came up from the midlands. Madge's sisters, Catherine and Angela, were matrons of honour, and she had three bridesmaids as well. Women shoppers stood in their dozens along the churchyard railings while photographs were taken on the sun-dappled lawn. Afterwards, a string of hired limousines and private cars drove fifteen miles to Beech Hall Country Club, which was known for the skill with which it handled private functions such as this. The champagne flowed without stint and those guests who, having travelled some distance, had eaten early or not at all sat down to the wedding breakfast in a fuddled but happy state of mind. Adam Greenaway had spared nothing in giving his firstborn the last-to-be-married daughter a splendid send-off.

In the late afternoon, Madge and Edgar Collins drove to London where they stayed the night. The next morning they went on to Lydd and flew with their car to Le Touquet. From there they motored south, staying single nights in towns which took their fancy along the route:

Troyes, Dijon, Valence and finally Arles. They had intended to go right down on to the Côte d'Azur, but Arles charmed them and thinking of the crowds they would find on the coast they decided to stay there until it was time for them to go north again. Apart from excursions into the countryside and to nearby towns the pattern of their days was quiet and leisurely. In the mornings they walked about the town, looking at the Roman remains and the shops, Edgar talking a lot about Gauguin and Van Gogh; in the evenings they ate dinner in a small but admirable restaurant they had found by the Rhone bridge, then drank liqueurs and coffee sitting at a pavement table outside one of the cafés along the Marseilles road. During the afternoons, in the fiercest heat of the day, they stayed in the hotel near the Place du Forum, lying naked on one of the two wide beds in their room, making love then sleeping, with the shutters open on to a small sunlit courtyard.

Observing the sensuality that frequent lovemaking had kindled in her after all the years of abstinence, Madge was both involved and detached. She knew that Collins was madly in love with her body, living in a state of heightened sexual awareness that the tautening of the line of her breast or the movement of her thighs under her light skirts could explode into urgent desire; and if she were to be proficient in satisfying him it was as well that she should enjoy it also. Yet even in the moments when they were most closely locked together there was a part of her which stood outside and observed it all as a performance. She observed and judged and found it satisfactory.

The old man Collins worked with died and Collins took over the business. His affairs began to prosper. He had for a long time chafed under the restrictions the old man's conservative attitude had imposed on the firm; now he began to strike out after more ambitious jobs, and get them. He designed a new bus station for the town where his office was, and a small shopping precinct with flats. He found bigger premises, hired more staff, and was called in as consultant to the Borough Surveyor's department when several blocks of multi-storey flats were planned for a slum-clearance area. Madge's judgement in marrying him was vindicated. Collins was known as a coming man, and, what was more, one who was getting on through his own energy and ability. Madge encouraged him at every step, and when it was advantageous for his professional and private lives to overlap she was there with her direct support, ever the courteous and discerning hostess. If some of their guests felt a certain abrasiveness behind her charm, it was a not unfitting complement to Collins' own quiet unassuming warmth. Others succumbed without reservation. 'A delightful couple.' 'He's lucky to have a wife like that. It's hard luck when a man starts to climb and his wife can't keep up.' 'They're so very polite to each other, too. I wonder if they're like that in private.'

They were. For by this time what the world saw of them together was virtually all there was to be seen.

Two years after their marriage, Madge Collins lost a child through a miscarriage in her third month. The bad time she suffered then and the warning of a specialist about the dangers of another pregnancy were enough to kill her already failing sexual appetite. It had been pleasant enough for a time, but even in those very early days when she had most enjoyed the act some fastidious side of her nature had recoiled from so blatant an offering of herself. Once – just once – when Collins had reached and exposed a nerve she had not known she possessed, what she remembered afterwards was not the ecstasy but, with shame, the moment when she had yelled, and reared under him, and he had seen her lost. So, little by little, during the subsequent years she discouraged their intimacies, and without encouragement Collins' desires, too, seemed to die.

But in this assumption she was mistaken, and the revelation of her error shook her as nothing ever had before.

116

When their guests had left on that evening Collins stood looking into the sitting-room fire while Madge plumped up cushions and emptied ashtrays before sinking into a chair and lighting the last cigarette of the day.

'What would you say if I told you I had a mistress?' Collins turned as he spoke.

She didn't think she could have heard him properly. She looked at him. Her heart had quickened its beat to an uncomfortable rate.

'Are you serious, Edgar?'

'What would you say?'

'I take it it *is* a hypothetical question?'

'Would you mind? I mean, we haven't been lovers for years now.'

'I certainly wouldn't share you with anyone.'

'Not even though she wouldn't be taking anything you want for yourself?'

'I'm your wife, Edgar. I want, and expect, my due.'

'You mean you must own all of me so that the parts you're not interested in you can accept or reject as you like.'

'You're talking in riddles, Edgar.'

'Was it really the fear of becoming pregnant that turned you away from me, or did you just never enjoy it as I did?'

'We had our . . . our time of passion; I thought we'd both settled happily into a relationship of affection and mutual respect.'

'I'm sorry,' Collins said. 'It's not good enough. And it's much too late to remedy it now. Perhaps at one time, if I'd been a bit more persistent . . . But I hated to think you were doing anything against your will. Humouring me. "Being nice," they call it, don't they?'

'So you're trying to tell me you've found consolation elsewhere?' She must keep calm; not let him suspect the panic growing in her.

'The question was – would you mind?'

'And I believe I answered that by saying I wouldn't share you.'

117

Collins rattled a box of matches on the mantelshelf with the tips of his fingers. 'No,' he said eventually. 'Neither will she, not any longer.'

'You mean there really is somebody? What are you telling me this for? Are you trying to punish me for something?'

'I'm coming round to telling you that I want to leave you.'

She was proud of herself. It was really admirable the way she held herself in, taking this bombshell with no more sign of distress than a deep sigh.

'Is she someone I know?'

'No.'

'How old is she?'

'Twenty-five.'

'Pretty?'

He shrugged. 'So-so.'

'Prettier than I am?'

'It's not the point.'

'Younger, anyway.'

'That's not the point, either. I love her.'

'You used to say you loved me.'

'Oh, yes, I did.'

'But not any more?'

'I'm not satisfied with the way our marriage has gone, Madge. There was a time when I thought that if only I could get you there'd be nothing I couldn't do. But it's sterile – all surface show, appearances.'

'You miss not having children?'

'I do, of course I do, but that wouldn't have mattered so much if I'd still had you.'

'You've got me. I'm not the one who's talking of leaving.'

'Madge, we don't live together, we live side by side.'

'I just don't know how we've come to this, Edgar. I never realized, not for one moment, that you were so . . . so unhappy.'

'It happened gradually,' Collins said, 'through all the years when you pulled away from me and into yourself.

Even before that; even in the very early days when just some little unconscious movement would make me tremble with wanting you. Even then I knew there was a part of you holding back. As though you felt you'd lose something absolutely vital to yourself if you ever really gave yourself up to me. Marriage to you is a social convenience. I don't think you were ever capable of the kind of relationship I hoped for and needed.'

'Thank you for telling me. What do you intend to do?'

'Leave here, give you the evidence you need, and ask you to divorce me.'

'Where will you go?'

'I have a flat. I've had it for some time. It's furnished and ready for me to move into.'

'My God, Edgar, you have got it all worked out, haven't you? Well, go and live in your little love-nest and take her with you; but if you plan to marry her you'd better tell her she'll have to wait a long time, because you'll get no divorce from me.'

'I hoped you'd see it more reasonably than that.'

'Did you expect my blessing?'

'Madge, you're like a selfish child with a cupboard full of dolls. You don't play with most of them but you wouldn't dream of giving them to someone more needy than yourself.'

'*I* need you. Does that satisfy you?'

'You need me for what? Look, I'm a living, breathing human being. I want someone I can cling to, who'll cling to me. I want *warmth*, Madge, and tenderness. I want *love*, not a social contract, an arrangement for the eyes of the world. I'm stifling, Madge, and I want *life*.'

'And I? What do I get?'

'You've got yourself,' he said. 'You've taken good care of that, and it's all you've ever needed.'

Collins left the house early next morning to drive to a business appointment in Birmingham. Madge stayed in bed until he'd gone. She had slept only fitfully, coming awake after each shallow spell to shocking awareness of the catastrophe which faced her. Always, at every

119

stage of her life, she had felt herself capable of controlling matters to her satisfaction. What she could not mould or shape to her image of what was fitting and proper for her she had avoided with an unerring instinct. And now, to be led to this pass . . . The humiliation of it seared her. She coloured up, her cheeks flaming, as she pondered the implications of it. She was supposed to lunch with a friend but she telephoned and cried off, giving a bad headache as her excuse; she did not, for once, feel herself capable of getting through the occasion without betraying something of what she was feeling. And no-one must know. Not a soul must entertain the slightest suspicion that all wasn't well, until she had had time to think what she could do.

Sometime about mid-morning she went into her husband's study. There was a drawing-board on a flat table, a couple of filing cabinets, and a divan bed that Collins had often slept on when working late at night. He had slept there last night and the rumpled sheets were thrown back as he had left them. She looked at the roll-top desk where he kept personal papers. It was locked. She was consumed with curiosity about the girl. Would she, if she broke open the desk, find something she could defend herself with? No, she would not be seen to lose control in that vulgar way.

Collins would not be back until late. There was nothing she could do until she could talk to him again, try some different approach, make promises, get him to see reason. Plead with him, if it came to that. Yes, she would plead. Would he realize then, when she begged him, that she too was a human being with needs outside herself? And what would be left of her then, when she had so humbled herself? She clenched her fists and beat them at the air in her exasperation.

She tried to read. Then she sat before the television set during the afternoon's schools' programmes, smoking incessantly. Later, she did a little desultory housework. She had not been out of the house, feeling that her dilemma was written across her face for all the world to see. She had made lunch of an apple and a glass of milk; now she cooked herself an omelette and ate it at the kitchen table.

She didn't believe it; that was her trouble. She just didn't believe it was happening to her.

At seven the doorbell rang. There was a police sergeant on the step.

'Mrs Collins?'

'Yes.'

'Mrs Edgar Collins?'

'That's right.'

'I wonder if I could come in for a minute, Mrs Collins. It's about your husband.'

She led the way into the sitting-room, then turned to face him. 'What it is?' It came to her as she spoke. 'Has there been an accident?'

'I'm afraid so, Mrs Collins. Nottinghamshire County Constabulary came through to us just now. A pile-up on the M1. Eight cars involved, one of them your husband's.'

'You've no idea how—?'

'I have a number for you to ring. It's the hospital they took him to.'

'And you've no idea whether he's badly hurt?'

'You ring that number, Mrs Collins. I'll hang on a minute while you do.'

She went to the telephone. Collins was gravely ill, a woman's voice told her. Yes, she could go down if she wished but she would be able to look at him for only a minute or two, and he would not know her, because he was unconscious.

She rang off and 'phoned her father. Adam Greenaway came straight over to pick her up.

They spoke little as they went south down the motorway, except for one exchange when Adam Greenaway said:

'I heard it on the six o'clock news. Listened to 'em and thought nothing of it. Eight cars. Rain after a dry spell. Greasy road. Somebody going too fast and can't pull up

121

in time. Then you've got a pile-up. People get hurt in cars every day, yet you somehow never think of it happening to someone close.' He grunted. 'No, that's not right. You always think of it happening to someone close, never to yourself. I remember when you and Catherine were still at home, how on edge I'd be when you were out in the car in doubtful weather. But Edgar's such a damned good driver. Fast, but as safe as houses.'

'You can't always account for the other person,' Madge said.

'No, that you can't. Too many damned maniacs on the road nowadays. There was a time when driving was a pleasure. Not any more. D'you know, I've been on the motorway and actually had chaps pass me *on the inside*?'

An hour later they stood in turn at the porthole window of an intensive care room and looked at what they could see of Edgar Collins lying inside the shiny transparent skin on an oxygen tent. He could have been anybody. He had multiple injuries, the sister said, and they couldn't deny the gravity of his condition. Had they driven far?

Madge told her.

'It's a long way. Of course, you can visit when you like, but there's not much you can do until he recovers consciousness.'

'I shall come,' Madge said.

'Of course,' Adam Greenaway said. 'I shall bring you. Don't worry about that.'

'I should telephone in the morning and see if there's any change.'

Madge asked about Collins' personal effects. 'His keys in particular. They'll be needed for his business.'

'Yes, of course.'

The sister brought Collins' things and Madge signed for them.

'You're sure you'll be all right on your own?' Adam Greenaway asked when he drew up at her door. 'Wouldn't you rather come home for a day or two?'

'I shall be all right,' Madge said. 'In any case, I gave them this phone number to ring if there's any news.'

She went in, took off her coat, and smoked a cigarette before going upstairs with the keys and into Collins' study. She opened the roll-top desk and went through the papers. Most of them concerned matters she already knew about: Collins had kept no business secrets from her and they had regularly discussed the contracts he was working on. Then she found what she was looking for: a large square envelope containing letters from a woman, addressed to Collins at his office and marked 'personal'. She expressed regret that when she had fallen in love it had to be with a married man. It was up to him. If he said go away, leave him alone, she would; but not before he said it. Another letter was from a seaside town where she was on holiday. She was missing Collins badly, imagining him there, their having dinner together, then walking on the beach in moonlight . . . Madge's mouth curled. How the girl had thrown herself at him, blatantly, without reservation. Where was her pride? How had she known he wasn't just using her for a brief period of amusement? And then, once she was sure of him, the screw was turned:

'. . . if there were children involved I wouldn't say these things; but there's only you and her, and she can more than take care of herself. How long are we to go on like this, wasting our chances of happiness together while the years slip steadily by? I want to give you children and I don't want to leave it too late. You say you'll speak to her. Do it. Settle it. Come to me and I'll be everything you'll ever need . . .' There was a photograph too; it showed the face of a reasonably good-looking dark-haired girl who smiled slightly at the camera. Madge put everything away and had a hot bath. Then she drank some whisky and took a couple of sleeping-pills and went to bed.

There was no change in Collins' condition when she rang the hospital in the morning. He was still unconscious, and seriously ill. She drove down with her father again in the evening. The sister they had seen before brought a doctor to speak to Madge. He took her on one side.

'I'm sorry to have to tell you, Mrs Collins, but the situation is very grave.'

'He's not improving at all?'

The man shook his head. 'There's damage to the brain as well, you see. We might relieve that a little if we operated, but it's major surgery and in his condition he just couldn't stand it.'

'I see. So . . .'

'He's slipping, losing his hold. We're doing everything we can, but . . .' He shrugged regretfully.

'How long?'

'Now that's hard to say. He could surprise us all and—'

'Twenty-four hours?' Madge said. 'A couple of days?'

She went back to her father. 'Bad?' She nodded.

'You can take me home tonight, but first thing in the morning I shall pack a bag and drive back and book in at an hotel. I want to be near.'

'As bad as that?' Adam Greenaway said.

The telephone was ringing as Madge let herself into the house. She ran to it. A young woman's voice asked:

'Mrs Collins?'

'Speaking.'

'Could you tell me how Mr Collins is, please?'

'Who is that?' Madge said.

'I don't think it . . . I'm a friend of his. They told me at his office which hospital he was in, but when I rang them they were rather evasive.'

'They don't hold out any hope,' Madge said clearly. 'They think he's going to die.'

Madge heard a long shuddering sigh on the line. She waited. In a moment the girl said:

'I wonder if . . . You see, I don't think they'll let me—'

Madge cut her short. 'I'm afraid that's out of the question.' She replaced the receiver.

*

Edgar Collins died twenty-seven hours later, early in the morning. Madge was in the room when it happened. There was no change that she could discern and she recognized the moment only when the sister, who was checking apparatus on the other side of the bed, suddenly peered intently at Collins then hurried out to get the doctor. He came in, looked at what the sister had seen, then lifted up the side of the transparent tent to lean over the bed. He straightened up and turned to Madge.

'I'm sorry, Mrs Collins. I'm afraid he's gone.'

Madge got up off the chair in the corner and approached the bed. 'Can I look at him now?'

Adam Greenaway took over the arranging of the funeral in consultation with the friend whom Collins had named as executor of his estate. Before giving this man access to Collins' papers Madge took out of the desk the letters and the photograph of the girl. She tore them into small pieces and burned them on the sitting-room fire. She informed the managers of both of Collins' offices that they were to close on the day of the funeral. Then she took her address book and wrote and posted a large number of black-edged cards.

On the funeral morning Madge, dressing alone in her room, looked out of the window at the many cars standing in the drive and along the street. The voices of people calling to pay their respects before the coffin left the house had been heard in the hall for an hour or more. Adam Greenaway was receiving them but soon now she would have to go down and face them herself.

She sat down at her dressing-table and applied just a touch of almost colourless lipstick to her mouth. She wore no other make-up. Her hairdresser had visited the house yesterday, as had her dressmaker three days before. Now Madge took her hat and placed it on her head. Composedly, she looked at herself in the glass.

It was odd, she thought, how appropriate to one's nature the turns of life could be. Not that she was glad of Edgar's death. She would miss him a great deal. But she had been about to lose him anyway. And she could never have seen herself as a divorced or deserted woman. Everything in her recoiled from the picture. It cast doubt upon her, put her into an area of fallibility, in which she could be judged and possibly found wanting. Divorced? they would have said, their minds speculating. No matter that she would have been the innocent party; people would accept the legal apportioning of blame while nevertheless wondering how much and in what way she herself had been at fault. But bereavement and widowhood . . . these she could bear, and earn the admiration of her friends for her fortitude in the face of a blow from a malign providence. And her dignity.

She got up, made a last appraisal of herself in the full-length glass, and went out of her room and along the landing to the head of the stairs. She paused then, looking down at the people in the hall. Her presence communicated itself to most of them and they turned to watch her as, steadily, she began to descend. It came to her clearly then, in a thought too private – too harsh even – ever to be revealed. But she could not hide its precise expression from herself, for every face turned up to her was evidence of its truth. She was saved.

A Bit of a Commotion

There was a bit of a commotion in the bus station this morning. An old woman, crossing between two islands, got herself knocked down by a double-decker swinging in from the street. I was near enough to it but I didn't actually see anything, standing there reading the paper, hunched into the collar of my coat against the cold. Soon enough there are people bending over her and others craning their necks to see. An inspector makes his way across from a bus he's just boarded and he's joined by a second one from the office. They push their way into the middle and in a few seconds the one from the office is out again and going back where he came from, at a trot.

I watch a chap in overalls leave the scene and come over to join the queue I'm in.

'What's going on?'

'It's an old woman. Got knocked down.'

'You'd think they'd have more sense than to wander about out there.'

'Nay, some of them buses come in at a rare lick.'

'Is she hurt bad?'

'They can't tell. She's unconscious. They're debating whether to move her or leave her there till the ambulance comes.'

'Them buses come round that corner too fast,' a woman says.

'Well, you know that, so you've to take care.'

'She's nobbut an old woman.'

'So if she's short-sighted or hard of hearing, and not so nimble, she ought to take more care.'

127

'You'll be old yourself one day,' the woman says to me.
'Aye, happen so.'

'She's *somebody's* mother,' the woman mutters, which strikes me as a bloody silly thing to say. After all, it's the old woman herself who's laid out there, not her son or her daughter.

'Let's hope it doesn't throw the services back,' I say, and I wish I hadn't then because I catch a couple of looks which show they're thinking I'm a right hard case. But I was just speaking my thoughts aloud. Because it would be just my luck that it's happened this morning, when I've turned over a new leaf. I'll get no mercy from Etherington, old woman or no old woman. He's told me about being late often enough and yesterday's was his final warning.

'One more time this month, Gravener, and you're out. Five minutes or half an hour won't make any difference. You'll be finished. I mean it. Absolutely and posi-tively. Out.' He walks away, and turns back. 'And don't think you can get round it by taking the day off. I shall be satisfied with nothing less than a doctor's note.'

So one day means taking a week and convincing a doctor that I'm badly. And no money except a couple of days' sick pay.

Phyllis is no help, the idle cow. No getting up for her half an hour before me and chivvying me about and sending me out with a good hot breakfast. Turning over for another hour's kip is all she's good for; that and queening it down at the pub every night. Still, I was the one who fell for her sharp tits, her long legs, and that 'come and get me if you're big enough' look. I shan't get another job with as much money as this one; and we need every penny we can get, believe you me, the way she can spend it.

So I'm standing there getting more and more worked up while the crowd's still gathered in the middle of the station and the buses are held up outside until the ambulance arrives. I know I should have come for an earlier bus still, and given myself twenty minutes to spare; but it's too late to think about that now. It's too late for everything except going back home and collecting my money and cards on Friday. We're not on the clock at our place but there's no getting past Etherington standing in that yard at eight sharp and seeing that everybody's in.

There's nobody downstairs when I get back home. Phyllis turns over in bed to look at me when I've stamped up the stairs.

'Don't you ever get out o' bed till dinnertime?'

'What you doing back here?'

'There's been an accident in the bus station. Everything's running late.'

'Well, couldn't you go, and tell 'em?'

'You know I told you I'd had my last warning.'

'What are you doing now, then?'

'I've come back. I'll fetch me money and cards on Friday.'

'You an' your turning over new leaves,' she says.

'A lot of bloody help you've been. A right wife 'ud have been up to send me off right. Anyway, I've told you, it's not my fault.'

'You're old enough to look after yourself. Only you can't do owt right, can you?'

'I did the first thing wrong when I wed you, you useless cow.'

'You know what you can do if you don't like it.'

'Aye! An' I'll start now.'

I grab the bedclothes and uncover her with one heave; then as she starts to struggle up I lace into her, slapping her about the bed till her yells and curses give way to tears. Then I stop and stand back, looking at her, half satisfied, half sorry at what I've done.

In a while she stops crying, twists on the bed, and gets up.

'No man does that to me, Harry Gravener.'

'One just has.'

'Aye, and it's the bloody last time.'

I leave her and go downstairs where I put the frying-pan on the ring, thinking that now I've the time I might as well at least have a right breakfast. I've got everything nicely sizzling and popping and a pot of tea on the brew when Phyllis comes down, dressed to go out and with a little case in her hand.

'Where d'you think you're going?'

'Out. And I shan't be back.'

'If you can find a better hole than this, get off to it. There isn't another feller who'd put up with your ways for a week.'

'Thanks. We shall see.'

I turn back to the cooker and hear the door shut behind her, which takes me aback a bit because I didn't expect her to go without a bit more argument. If she went at all. I sit down and get on with my bacon and eggs, thinking she'll be back.

There's no sign of her by eight o'clock. But I've already decided that I'll give her a day or two to cool down and come to her senses before I make any move to look for her.

I go down to the pub for want of something better to do and one of the first people I see is Walt Henshaw from the yard.

'What's been up with you today, then? Badly?'

'Oh, I didn't feel so well this morning so I laid in.'

'You'd better have another couple, then, and get a sick note for Etherington.'

'Bugger Etherington, and his job an' all.'

'I thought you were late again when you didn't turn up at eight.'

'I expect Etherington thought that an' all. I can just see him standing there rubbin' his hands an' waiting to finish me.'

'No, he wasn't there to watch for latecomers today. He no sooner got there than he was called away again, by a phone call.'

'Oh?'

'Aye. It was his mother. Seems she got knocked down in the bus station this morning.'

The Assailants

The ten-tonner with the man working under it by the glow of the wire-caged inspection light stood, parked pretty, on the almost empty patch of waste ground.

Brian had left Aberdeen late yesterday, after a half-day's search for a return load, and limped into here in the small hours, to spend what was left of the night in searching for the fault in his engine and repairing it as best he could with the tools to hand. Now he was done. He pulled himself out with a grunt and stood upright, wiping his hands on a piece of rag. The sky had lightened quite quickly while he was under the vehicle and he glanced about him at the shabby streets of silent houses and wondered whether he should break the quiet with a trial start of the engine.

He decided against it. Let them have the rest of their sleep till the early traffic began. The engine would get him home. He was good with engines and he would never have left the motor repair shop had his boss, Nevinson, not driven him beyond the limit of his good nature and Joyce, in temper, persuaded him to stick up for his rights. The lorries were something that came his way almost immediately and Joyce had got him to take them as a temporary measure while he looked round for another place. But he'd been driving for a couple of years now; he was a steady man and he didn't like to chop and change.

There was a raw dampness in the air and it chilled him as, the concentration and effort of his task over, he stood there beside the lorry, thinking about what he ought to do, the rag working in the almost unconscious movements of his hands. Finally he closed the cowling over the engine and took his donkey jacket out of the cab before locking the door and walking with steady strides, a big man, out of the park. The sodium lights on their tall, bird's-neck standards of concrete were switching off in batches all the way down the long main road into the city, the pink glow of the fading filaments lingering against the pallid dawn sky. Brian crossed over towards a house next to a small general shop. He had his hand on the doorknob when an approaching motor-bike cleaved the quiet he had been reluctant to disturb with a bandsaw rasp of brutal unsilenced sound. He stood for a moment and watched it go by, the black-clad rider crouched low over short swept-back handlebars, and his mouth moved with mild derision to frame the one word 'cowboy' before he opened the door and went into the house.

The sound of the door brought Mrs Sugden out of the bathroom and down on to the half-landing, a thick blue dressing-gown over her nightclothes.

'Good heavens, it's you, Brian. I thought you were in bed and asleep hours since. Have you been out there all this time?'

'It took longer than I expected.'

'I should think so. And me lying up there half the night with the door unlocked for anybody to walk in that fancied.'

'I was only across the street.'

'With your head stuck in that engine and taking no notice of anything else.'

She came down and passed him to go into the kitchen. He followed and watched her move the draught regulator on the coke-burning stove in the fireplace.

'I shouldn't ha' thought you'd be so timid,' he said. 'I mean, all the fellers 'at sleep here ...'

'I can size them up before I let 'em in,' Mrs Sugden said. 'But I can't do owt about somebody who walks in off the street in the middle of the night.'

Brian's lips moved in a faint smile. He didn't take her complaint seriously. He knew she was more concerned that he should have spent all that time across there in the cold when he could have been in a warm bed. She was like that with him; she thought that his nature saddled him with more inconvenience and discomfort than was necessary.

'Sit yourself down and get warm. I'll cook you some breakfast as soon as I've got dressed.'

He moved across the room and sank into a fireside chair, which had a loosely draped shroudlike cover over it to protect the upholstery from greasy overalls, and stretched out his legs towards the stove as Mrs Sugden left the room and went back upstairs. His presence in the kitchen made him the privileged of the privileged; for Mrs Sugden gave food and shelter with care, selecting only those she liked the look of, and most of the men she took in ate in the bare dining-room across the hall, with its formica-topped tables and easily scrubbed lino-covered floor. She had to be careful: he understood that. There were loudmouths in any pull-in, ready to brag about the extra comforts to be found along the road, and as a widow still, in her forties, handsome and well set-up, her motive in offering beds to men here today and gone tomorrow would, to some of them, appear more than the simple one of augmenting the living she made from the little general shop next door.

You had, indeed, Brian found, to be careful yourself as you moved about the country. Some men courted trouble in their readiness to accept casual pleasure. There was the place in Liverpool where that simple-faced teen-aged girl rubbed her breasts against any man she could get close to, going with some of them behind the vehicles in the lorry park when she had a few minutes free from waiting on tables. He'd an idea she was younger than her well-developed body and the sly carnality of her glance suggested. Sooner or later somebody would knock her up, or the police move in and start asking questions. So Brian had taken warning and not gone back. Then there were the birds you met along the road, hanging about the cafés waiting for lifts. Brian left them to the men who liked the possibility of a bit on the side in exchange for a ride, or the others whose only motive in helping them on their way was good nature. Singly or two together, they were all potential trouble and he kept clear of them.

His eyelids drooped in the rising heat from the stove and he woke some time later to the sizzle and smell of bacon frying on the cooker. Mrs Sugden was looking at him.

'Now then. You've just saved me from having to wake you. Your breakfast's nearly ready.'

'How long have I been asleep?'

'Oh, three-quarters of an hour, maybe. I did think at one time of leaving you; but when you've got some breakfast into you you can get off up into a comfortable bed.'

He sat up and knuckled his eyelids.

'I've just been thinking. I'll have me breakfast and get on me way.'

She stared at him. 'But you've had no sleep, man.'

'It's all right. I'll make it up later.'

'They're poor employers 'at won't allow a man some leeway when he's had a breakdown. It's not your fault you had trouble with your lorry, is it? Now you're going to drive all that way with no more than a cat-nap. You're not safe on the road, man.'

'I shall be all right. I was thinking, y'see. It just occurred to me, if I set off now I can cut across and drop me load in Carlisle and get back down home before Joyce goes out tonight. Then Gloria won't have to go next door to Mrs Miles's.'

Mrs Sugden's head tilted back so that she seemed to aim the disapproval of her glance along her nose.

'Oh, that's it. She's still messing about with the Houdini feller, is she?'

'Leonardo, he calls himself,' Brian said. 'That's his stage name. His real name's Leonard. Leonard Draper.'

Mrs Sugden turned to the cooker and spoke over her shoulder: 'Leonardo, Houdini, or Uncle Tom Cobleigh. I don't know as his name makes any difference.'

'She enjoys it. It gets her out and meeting people. What with me being away so much.'

'Aye, with that bairn pushed from pillar to post, and when you are at home you've got to sit on your own while she's out cavorting on a stage with a conjuror . . . You'd better get your hands washed. It's ready.'

He got up and went to the sink, standing next to her as he ran water and fingered grease-remover out of the tin she kept there. 'He's a hypnotist mainly. That's his big thing.'

'He seems to have hypnotized your wife all right. All I can say is, some women are lucky to have husbands 'at'll stand for it. My Norman wouldn't have had it. He thought a woman's place was in the home and I was content to abide by that. We were never lucky enough to have any kiddies, and I didn't take boarders in in them days, either; but I'd plenty to keep me occupied in making a nice home for him.'

He moved his shoulders in embarrassment. He regretted having told her about Joyce and Draper in that quiet conversation some months ago. It was from this that she had made her quick summing-up of him, fixing him immediately as a man who could be put upon. And, that lesson learned, he should have held his tongue just now and left without giving her more ammunition to fire at the wife she'd never met in her self-appointed role of defender of him, who was too soft for his own good. For she didn't understand, couldn't know. She was, in her own way, like some of the drivers he heard talking, men who were always bragging about some point scored, some small victory won over the missus; as though marriage were a never-ending battle in which any concession was a weakness to be exploited. It wasn't like that with him and Joyce.

'Anyway,' Mrs Sugden said, 'I'd've thought she'd see enough people working in the shop all day.'

'That's not the same thing. She likes being on the stage. It's . . . it's glamorous to her.'

'I'd give her glamorous. Showing herself off in front of all manner of folk. Her with a husband and a growing bairn.'

'Aw, you're old fashioned, Mrs Sugden. You think everybody should be like you.'

'Aye, I talk like your mother might, don't I? When there's less than ten years between us.' She put the plate of bacon and eggs on the table and clamped the fingers of one hand on to a loaf of bread, the knife poised in the other. 'Still, I like to think I've picked up a bit of sense over the years.'

'I suppose you'd have me stop her going out to work as well wouldn't you?'

'Why not? It'd make sense. Working for that feller during the day and going all manner of places with him at night. She must see ten times more of him than she does you.'

'It's not every night. And you can't be suggesting there's—'

'I'm suggesting nothing. I'm just seeing a carry-on that isn't all it should be. Come on, get it down before it goes cold.'

'Maybe I'm not all I should be,' Brian said.

'You what?' Her gaze came directly on to him again, the knife arrested this time half-way in its cut through the bread.

'Well, if I can't earn enough to keep us in all we want, and I'm only at home half the time, can you wonder she has to go out to work and wants a bit of . . . of excitement in her life?'

'Why, there's many a woman 'ud . . .' She stopped, as though on the verge of saying too much, and severed the slice from the loaf with two heavy strokes of the knife. 'What are you always underselling yourself for, you big daft lump?' Her voice fell as she turned away, and what she said came in a dismissive mutter, as if to end the conversation: 'You must be a daft lump or

136

you'd have told me to mind my own business by now.'

Yes, he would have to do that – or stop coming here. Which would be a pity, because it was a fine place, the best he knew. He glanced at her back briefly but she said nothing more. He took the slice of bread and dipped a corner of it into the soft yolk of the egg on his plate and began to eat.

'You'll be all right, then, Gloria, now your daddy's here.'

The little girl sat up close to Brian on the sofa, her eyes fixed on the bluish square of the television screen. A sudden loud burst of music made the picture tremble, the figures on it wavering as though seen through disturbed water.

'Oh, it's always doing that,' Gloria said. 'It spoils all the best parts. Can't you twiddle a knob or something, Daddy?'

'I've adjusted it all I can,' Brian said. 'It must be the aerial.'

'It's the set that's clapped out,' Joyce put in. 'It's time we had a new one.' She was looking distractedly round the room. 'Where did I put my hairbrush? You haven't had it, have you, Gloria? I'm talking to you, Gloria.'

'No, Mummy.'

Joyce began moving cushions. 'Here it is.' She stood on the hearthrug and brushed her hair in the glass over the fireplace. Among the pale gold were some strands that shone like silver as the light caught them. They were the lingering tints of childhood, not a sign of advancing years, but she was self-conscious about them and sometimes spoke of dyeing the whole to a uniform blonde. Brian was against it.

'I can't see, Mummy.'

'You'll have to do without for a minute. I'm late as it is.'

'Where is it tonight?' Brian asked.

'Forest Green Club.'

'Have they a good audience?'

'I don't know. If it's like most of the other workingmen's clubs all they want is singers and comedians.'

'Can I look at your costume, Mummy?' Gloria said.

'Oh, Gloria. It's every time I go out. You've seen it many a time, and I'm late, love.'

'Oh, come on, Mummy, just let me see it.'

'Well, if I do you'll promise to be good and not give your daddy any trouble about going to bed?'

'She's never any trouble. Are you, poppet?'

Joyce slipped off her skirt to reveal the glitter-finish stage costume, cut high up each groin to display the full length of her splendid legs in nylon mesh tights. She put one hand on her hip, throwing up the other one and turning slightly on one foot. 'Ta-rah!' At the same time she shot a quick sideways glance at Brian's face as though to detect any sign of disapproval. It was odd how the costume always seemed more excessive here in the confines of the house than it ever did on stage, making her self-conscious about this private display of limbs which, later, she would show without qualms to an audience of strangers.

'You do look lovely, Mummy.'

'Yes, I'm not wearing too badly, love. I can still make their heads turn.' She glanced down at her legs. 'A few pints and a look at them and Leonard can get away with murder.'

The flippancy of her remark compensated for that silly twinge of guilt. There was nothing brazen in what she did. And Brian didn't care, anyway. His face was impassive as his gaze ran briefly over her then switched back to the television screen. She reached for her skirt and finished getting ready to go.

By nine-thirty Leonardo had run through the first part of his act – the routine with coloured skills and steel rings which mysteriously linked themselves and came apart again – and, timing the audience's patience for this run-of-the-mill conjuring to a nicety, culminated it by producing Joyce from the interior of a dolls' house which he had just demonstrated as being empty. Now he came to his speciality, in which the audience would participate through identification with one or more of its members. Occasionally people quizzed Joyce about the secrets of Leonardo's act, ending, when she refused to be drawn, with the exclamation: 'Oh, well, we know they're all tricks'. Of course they were tricks! It was the skill with which he hid the trickery which made the routine. All that was, except the hypnotism. That was proved to be genuine every time he did it. Joyce had seen him put half the people in a room under, their fingers locked foolishly behind their necks until he released them. She herself had never seen her part of the routine they did together and could only believe it when, during their first rehearsals, he had taken a photograph and shown it to her afterwards. She'd not been able to suppress all feeling of uneasiness, but tried to cover it with a little laugh. 'There's no knowing what you could get me doing when I'm under,' she said. 'Oh, basically the subject won't do anything against his nature,' Leonard explained. 'On the other hand, who knows what urges are bottled up inside people? I once had a young woman on stage who showed an irresistible desire to take all her clothes off. I had to snap her out of that pretty quickly, or we'd have all been in trouble.'

The concert room of the club was almost full, with people sitting in groups of two, three and four at the small tables and waiters moving about between them and the long bar at the far end. Joyce always admired the assurance with which Leonard adapted himself to different audiences. All she had to do, mostly, was stand there and look attractive, handing him his props on cue while he pattered away, working his charm and reminding her with his immaculate evening clothes and sleek black hair of the rich society heroes of those Hollywood comedies of the late 'thirties in which the characters divided their time between lounging in de-luxe apartments and drinking champagne in an apparently endless series of night-clubs. She had, in the beginning, been thrown by his occasional muttered phrases of contempt when some inattentive or imperceptive audience missed the full appreciation of a clever routine; but she took that kind of thing in her stride now, never relaxing her own bright stage charm. The mild derision with which he judged the intelligence of most of the people he played to heightened the pleasure she got from being in league with him, the sharer of his professional secrets, the closest observer of his skill. With her he was always courteous: the best mannered man she had ever known. Being with him gave her a feeling of touching the fringe of a more gracious world and added to the excitement she derived from appearing on stage. She wondered, sometimes, whether he had any sex life, or if, as it seemed to her, his thoughts outside his business were entirely concentrated on perfecting his act and finding an audience before which he could really prove himself.

'And now, ladies and gentlemen, for the next part of our performance, which is a demonstration of the power of mind over matter, I need the assistance of a volunteer from the audience. A muscular young man . . . Have we any handsome specimen of British manhood who is willing to come forward and help me?'

There was a stir in the audience as people looked at their neighbours. Joyce picked out a table down front at which a young woman was nudging her companion with her elbow while he made grimaces of resistance. Leonard had spotted them too.

'Do I see someone down there trying to make up his mind? Come along, sir. Don't be shy.'

He turned his head and nodded to Joyce, who went down off stage to a greeting of shouts and whistles and held out her hand with a smile to the young man. The girl put both hands on his back and pushed. 'Go on with yer. What yer scared of?'

The boy shrugged in an elaborate attempt at casualness and let Joyce lead him up off the floor of the hall, Leonard starting a round of applause as, still held by Joyce's hand, he followed her on to the stage. She eyed him discreetly as he faced Leonard; not tall, but broad-shouldered and deep-chested: no waster.

'Now, sir,' Leonard began, 'let me first of all assure you that you'll be perfectly safe up here with us. Tell me, have you ever been hypnotized?'

'Not by a feller,' the boy said, and Leonard responded with his quick stage grin.

'Quite so. But have you any objection to my hypnotizing you now?'

'Not if you can.'

'You don't think I can? By the way, will you tell me your name?'

'Ted.'

'Right, Ted. You say you don't think I can put you under hypnosis.'

'Yes. I mean, no.'

'That's a pity. Hypnotism, you know, does rely a great deal on the willing co-operation of the subject. However, we'll do our best.' Leonard raised his right hand, the forefinger extended. There was a thimble on the end of it which flashed brilliantly in the lights. 'Would you keep your eyes fixed on the charm, Ted. I shall count to six. On the count of six I want you to close your eyes. I shall continue counting to twelve. On the count of twelve you will be under my influence. You will be able to hear what I say and acknowledge by nodding your head. Keep your eye on the charm . . .'

Ted's eyes closed on six and at twelve, when Leonard asked him if he could hear what he said, his head dutifully nodded.

'I want you to put your hands on top of your head and link your fingers.' As Ted obeyed Leonard turned away from him. 'I think he'll be quiet till we need him again.'

He waited till the laughter subsided. 'Now, ladies and gentlemen, to demonstrate further the marvellous power of mind over matter I am going to put my assistant, the charming Joyce, into a trance . . .'

She went under easily and, at Leonard's bidding, walked to where three straight chairs stood in a row and

141

lay down across them. Leonard made sure that her head and heels were in position.

'I am now going to remove the middle chair but you will remain supported in the same position.'

There was applause as Leonard took out the middle chair, leaving Joyce stretched rigid, supported only by her heels and the back of her head.

'We can leave her for a moment, ladies and gentlemen. I assure you she is quite comfortable and can rest like that indefinitely. Now back to our young friend . . .' He stood before Ted. 'On the count of three you will wake up but you will not be able to unlock your hands. One – two – three.'

Ted blinked as he came awake. He tried to lower his arms, but he couldn't. 'Here, what you done?'

'Can't you unlock your fingers?'

'No, I can't.'

'When I snap my fingers twice you will be able to.'

The girl Ted had left at the table laughed delightedly as he was released.

'Now,' Leonard said, 'I want you to observe my assistant.'

'Any time.'

'Yes, I know what you mean. Observe her, balanced between those chairs, supported only by her head and her heels. Do you think you could rest like that?'

'I expect you could make me.'

'I see we have a convert here, ladies and gentlemen. Tell me, Ted, how much do you weigh?'

'Thirteen and a half stone.'

'Do you think Joyce could support such a weight in the position she's in?'

'No, she'd collapse.'

'Shall we try it?'

'You mean me?'

'Yes, Ted, you.'

'I don't want to hurt her.'

'I can assure you that I'll take full responsibility . . . Ladies and gentlemen, such is the nature of the trance

142

I've imposed on my assistant she can do things she would not normally be capable of. This is the power of the prepared mind over the inadequacies of the body. Our friend tells me he weighs thirteen and a half stone. I shall now demonstrate that, under my influence, Joyce can support this weight. Now, Ted, come along with me. I want you to sit on Joyce.' Ted looked at Joyce then Leonard. 'It's all right; don't be shy. Give me your hands. Now, gently down on to her midriff . . . There. Are you comfortable?'

'More or less.'

'You won't fall over if I let go of your hands?'

'No.'

'Righto, then. When I let go of you I want you to lift your feet slowly off the floor until your full weight is resting on Joyce. All right.'

He released Ted's hands and the boy uneasily raised his feet.

'No wires and no invisible aids, ladies and gentlemen. Joyce is now carrying thirteen and a half stone on her unsupported body. Try it when you get home, ladies and gentlemen. But put some cushions on the floor first . . . Thank you, ladies and gentlemen. Thank you, Ted. A round of applause for Joyce, ladies and gentlemen, as I free her from her trance.'

He replaced the third chair and snapped his fingers. Joyce opened her eyes and sat up, swinging round to stand on her feet. Ted said something to Leonard, who stepped closer to him and listened.

'Ladies and gentlemen, our young volunteer has asked me if I can stop him smoking. Do you really want to stop?'

'Yes, I do.'

'And have you tried to do it for yourself?'

'I've had one or two goes.'

'But without success?'

'The trouble is, I like it too much.'

'Ah, yes, quite so. Well, since you've helped me so splendidly this evening I'll see what I can do. I shall put you under my influence first. Please look closely at the

143

charm again. Again, when I've counted to six you will close your eyes. At the count of twelve you will be under my control . . .' Leonardo put him under and glanced at his watch. 'At ten-fifteen you will light a cigarette. That cigarette will taste revolting and you will put it out. Cigarettes will continue to taste revolting and you will lose all desire to smoke them. Now when I snap my fingers twice you will awake. You will not remember what I've said but you will act upon my commands.'

'Is that it?' Ted asked a moment later.

'That's all, sir. Thank you very much. A big hand for a good sport, ladies and gentlemen.'

A man in the passage lurched into Joyce's path as they went down off the stage. 'That was lovely, darlin'. Just lovely.' Her reaction as his hands fell on her shoulders was to push him away so hard that he lost his balance and reeled back against the wall.

'That's not part of the act, mister.'

The man blinked his eyes several times in something like surprise. 'My sincere apologies, darlin'. No offence meant. Absolutely not.' He straightened up and walked towards the door, still talking. 'Wouldn't dream of it . . .'

'Stupid devil,' Joyce said. She turned to see the sardonic amusement in Leonard's eyes.

'You don't give them much change, do you?'

'Ah, you show them your legs and they think they can maul you.'

'You're a little puritan. I've told you before.'

'Maybe I am. It's my privilege, though.'

He smiled. 'Go and get your clothes on and we'll go round for a drink.'

' ". . . the little girl was very frightened as she went along the dark corridor. Then suddenly she turned a corner and saw a light coming through a doorway. She made her way towards it and, lo and behold, there she found herself looking into a magnificent room. There was an enormous polished floor, paintings on the walls, and beautiful silk curtains at the windows. And all this

144

splendour was lit by the light from six huge blazing crystal chandeliers which hung from the painted ceiling. The little girl gasped at the wonder of it all. Where could she possibly be? And who could this magnificent room belong to?'' '

Brian closed the book. 'Do you know who it belonged to?'

'No,' Gloria said.

'Well, we'll find out tomorrow night.'

'Oh, Daddy, read me a bit more.'

'No. If it was on the telly you'd have to wait to find out, wouldn't you? And it's long past your bedtime. You'll be too tired to go to school in the morning.'

'Mrs Miles lets me stop up.'

'Well, she ought to know better.'

'What time will Mummy be coming home?'

'Not for a while yet.'

'Will you ask her to come and tuck me up?'

'I'll tell her. But if you're not asleep by then I shall be cross with you.'

'She's a lovely mummy, my mummy is.'

'Yes.'

She reached up and encircled his neck with her arms. 'And you're a lovely daddy as well.'

'I'm glad you think so. Now snuggle down and shut your eyes. I want you to be asleep in five minutes.'

Leonard glanced at his watch when he'd ordered the drinks. He touched Joyce's elbow as they stood at the long bar and indicated Ted sitting at his table. The boy took out a packet of cigarettes and said something to the girl he was with as he became aware of her and the people round them watching him. He lit a cigarette and took one pull before making a face and reaching for the ashtray. There was audible laughter from those sitting nearest to him and when the girl had spoken to him Ted looked over to where Leonard was standing and grinned, lifting his hand in a thumbs-up sign. Leonard acknowledged him and the small ripple of applause with a nod of the head and a slight smile as the club's entertainments secretary, a stocky grey-haired man with scarred thick-fingered hands, came to them.

'On the house, Mr . . . er . . .' he said as the barman placed their drinks on the counter.

'Thank you.' Leonard poured tonic water into Joyce's gin and added water to his own scotch.

'That was very good,' the secretary said. 'Very successful, I thought.' He handed Leonard an envelope. 'I think you'll find that right.'

Leonard took the envelope with some distaste at being paid in public and pocketed it without looking inside. 'Thank you.'

'They don't usually go for conjurors and suchlike,' the man said.

'I'm a hypnotist and illusionist,' Leonard said.

'Eh? Well, you know what I mean. And the young lady helped a lot. They all understand that kind of thing.'

'I know what you mean,' Leonard said. 'Any bunch of lads with a couple of guitars and a lot of cheek can hold them better than I can. It's too much trouble for them to watch a real artiste at work.'

'We're very selective in our bookings, y'know. We don't engage rubbish.'

'You certainly haven't in my case. Quality is still quality, even in these days when we seem to have less and less sense of real values.'

The man was beginning to look flustered. 'Yes, I'm sure we all appreciate—'

'No, I'm sorry,' Leonard said, 'but I don't think you do. What you've had tonight is as good as you'll get in the profession. I have a reputation, built up carefully over the years, and I'm proud of it. I don't care to expose it to those people who can't appreciate what they're seeing. Perhaps you've never heard of the W.C.M.?'

'No, I, er . . .'

'The World Conference of Magicians. It's to be held in Brighton in a few weeks' time. When you get on the stage there you're performing for your peers, not for an audience with one eye on you and the other on the waiter bringing the drinks. I hope with the help of my young lady assistant to come away with a few honours myself this year.'

'We must wish you luck, then, Mr, er, Leonardo. Excuse me. There's somebody over there I've got to talk to.'

His smile was strained as he left them.

'You went for him a bit hard, didn't you?' Joyce said.

'I will not be patronized by little runts like that.'

'He meant well enough.'

'So did that chap in the passage. We're all touchy in our different ways.'

'All right.'

'Would you like another drink?'

'I've got enough with this one, thanks. Anyway, I mustn't be late.'

'Don't worry. I can't see me sticking round this place for long.' He spoke to the barman. 'Another scotch, please.'

Joyce poured the rest of the tonic water into her glass and said, 'It's not on, you know, Leonard.'

'What isn't?'

'Brighton.'

'You mean he's put his foot down?'

'No.'

'Oh, my God, there's only three weeks to go and here you are, backing out on me.'

'I never said I'd go.'

'No, but I did think—'

'I'm a married woman, Leonard. I've got a husband and a child, I can't just slope off to Brighton for three or four days.'

'Look, I'm depending on you. I can do big things this year. I know I can. But not without you.'

'Can't you get somebody else?'

'Find somebody and train her in three weeks? Talk sense, love.'

147

'I'm sorry, Leonard. But you knew when I started what the position was.'

'I thought this was the middle of the twentieth century, not the nineteenth.'

'He puts up with a lot, you know.'

'And so he should. Look, would you like to go?'

'Of course I would. Three or four days at the seaside. And you know I like being in the act.'

'Ask him, then. Ask him tonight.'

'Look, it's—'

Leonard's fingers gripped her elbow and his eyes looked directly into hers. 'Ask him.'

He was asleep when she got home, sprawled in the chair in his working-clothes, his mouth slightly open. She switched off the television set and shook him by the shoulder.

'I just shut my eyes for a minute,' he said as he came awake. 'What time is it?'

'A quarter past eleven. Did Gloria go off all right? She wasn't fretful, was she?'

'No. Why?'

'I'd a feeling she might be sickening for something earlier today. Might have been my imagination. Have you had any supper?'

'No.'

'Do you want some now?'

'I don't know.' He rubbed his eyes and pulled himself up in the chair. 'Let's have a cup of tea while I think about it.'

She took off her coat and laid it across a chair and went into the kitchen. He followed her and stood in the doorway, stretching, as she filled the kettle.

'Ugh! It feels more like a quarter past three.'

'You should have gone to bed.'

'Ah, it gets till it's all bed and work. I don't see anything of you.'

'I know you hate it,' she said.

'What?'

'Me going out like this. Helping Leonard.'

'I've never said so, have I?'

'I know it, without you saying anything.'

'If it gives you a bit of pleasure, excitement. I mean, I'm away so much . . . It's no fun for you.'

'Are you going up north again tomorrow?'

'No, he's putting me on local runs for a day or two, till he gets the wagon properly seen-to.'

The kettle was on the gas. She put tea into the pot and set out two cups. 'Do you want something to eat, then? I might as well see to it while I'm here.'

'Go on, then,' he said. 'I'll have a bacon sandwich.'

Joyce put the frying pan on another ring and took bacon out of the cupboard. She kept her eyes on her hands trimming off the rind as she said, 'Leonard's talking about the World Conference now.'

'What conference?'

'World Conference of Magicians. Didn't I mention it? I knew it was out of the question, anyway. Brighton, in three weeks' time. He reckons he can sweep the board if I'm there to help him.'

'Brighton?'

'Yes. Isn't it silly? Three or four days away. I told him, what did he expect? Me, a married woman, with a husband and a little girl to think about.'

'You're not going, are you?'

'Well, of course, I told him.'

'You want to go, though, don't you? You'd like to go with him?'

'What do you mean "with him"? Have I asked you?'

'You're asking me now.'

'Look. I—'

'You're not going.'

'Look, Brian, don't come the heavy husband with me. There's no need for you to lay the law down.'

'I want him to know,' Brian said. 'I want you to tell him.'

'Tell him what he knows already? Or that you've put your foot down?'

'I don't care. Just tell him.'

'Look, Brian, just who the hell do you think you are?'

'I'm your husband.'

'And how long do I have to go on being grateful for that?'

'I don't know what you mean.'

'You should. I was grateful when you married me. Not every man would have done what you did, would they? You took me and made me respectable. You got me out of trouble. Why shouldn't I have been grateful?'

'I married you because I loved you.'

'Because you wanted to go to bed with me and I was carrying somebody else's kid.'

'There's no need for talk like that.'

'Would you like to forget it? Don't you think about it every time you look at her? She's upstairs now, asleep. She doesn't know, but we do. When shall we tell her, Brian?'

'It was a long time ago. She's eight years old now and she's ours – yours and mine. Why do you want to start on all this?'

'Because I'm sick of it. Sick of everything.'

'You wouldn't tell her, would you?'

She faced him. 'Why not? Hasn't she got a right to know the truth?'

'There we are, sir. And your receipt. Your suit will be packed up and waiting for you when you call back. I hope you'll find it satisfactory in every respect.'

Leonard's customer smiled. 'I'm sure I shall. I must say it's a pleasure to shop where there's still some service.'

'It's very kind of you to say so, sir. Quality and courtesy are the cornerstones of any good business.'

'There's a lot of people forgotten that, though.'

'There are indeed, sir. There are indeed.' He opened the door for the man. 'Good day, sir.'

He picked up the suit from the counter and went into the back room where Joyce, with cups and teapot ready, was waiting for the electric kettle to boil.

'Nicely timed. I'm just brewing up.'

150

'I'll just pack this and we'll have a nice cuppa.'

'He seemed very pleased, the man who's just gone out.'

'We're both pleased. That makes for a satisfactory transaction.'

'You're a good tailor, aren't you, Leonard?'

Leonard brushed the suit down with the flat of his hand, holding it up for a last scrutiny before folding it into a large square box which he then tied round with string. 'The best in this town.'

'Haven't you ever thought of expanding? You know, opening another shop?'

'I did consider it at one time. But I couldn't be in two places at once and I didn't fancy the idea of putting my reputation into the hands of somebody who might not care for it as I do. So I settled for one shop and that run well. It works. I'm well known to a good clientele and I make a comfortable living. Personal service from the man who actually cuts the cloth – that's what they expect and what they're prepared to pay for.'

Joyce poured boiling water into the teapot. 'Leonard, about the conference.'

'Yes?'

'It's still no go.'

'You asked him, then?'

'No, I didn't actually ask him. I told him it was coming off. He jumped on it straight away. We had a row.'

'I'm sorry.'

'It was my fault, I suppose. I lost my temper and said some awful things.'

'He never...' Leonard hesitated. 'He doesn't strike you, does he?'

'Brian?'

'He's a big strong ox of a man. They do lose themselves sometimes.'

'The trouble with Brian is he won't argue or row. That's what makes me so mad sometimes. The way he stands there so bloody good and patient.'

'And stupid,' Leonard said.

'What?'

'Yes, I'm sorry, Joyce – stupid. Doesn't he realize what sort of woman you are? That you deserve something better than being tied to the house, cooking and cleaning for him?'

'Don't all women think like that sometimes?'

'There are plenty of women who are happy with that. They're ten a penny. But you're special, something different. You're like a lovely tropical bird that loses its colours and dies when it can't spread its wings and fly.'

She suppressed her desire to laugh at this sudden fanciful flight of talk.

'A bird in a gilded cage. Except the cage isn't gold. It's all very well, but—'

'No, Joyce.' He came round the table and took her hands. There was something in his eyes that she'd never seen before. 'It just won't do.'

She was so surprised then, when he kissed her, that she rested passively and without resistance in his arms. Until the pressure of his embrace increased, when she pulled free with a light laugh.

'Why, Leonard, I never knew you were one for kissing and cuddling in the back room.'

He held her hands. 'Joyce, I've never said anything before. I thought I'd no right. But I can't stand around and watch it any longer. You, grubbing for extra money, living a life with no beauty or refinement in it. I'm not a wealthy man but I could give you at least something of what you ought to have. A better life than you'll ever have with him.'

She withdrew her hands and tried to hide her surprise and confusion by pouring the tea. 'You've given me a shock,' she said eventually.

'I've always hidden it before,' he said. 'As I say, I didn't think I'd the right. You should know as well that I . . . I shouldn't make any demands that you weren't prepared to accept.'

It had gone far enough. She said with a little dismissive laugh. 'Don't talk silly.'

He stiffened, not answering.

'I'm sorry, Leonard. You just don't understand.'

'I can understand misplaced loyalty. I know what sort of woman you are, I wouldn't want you if you were any other way.'

'It's loyalty, Leonard, but it's not misplaced. And it's something more than that.'

'You can't tell me you still love him.'

'I said some things to him last night, and afterwards, when I saw the look on his face, I could have killed myself.'

'You don't like to hurt people. What you don't realize is that it's not you but the truth that does the damage.'

'I did a terrible thing. I threw it in his face that Gloria isn't his child. After all these years.'

'What? What do you mean?'

'She isn't his. You didn't know that, did you? I had an affair with a married man. I was young and silly, I suppose. Anyway, I'd finished it just before I met Brian and not long after I'd started going out with him I realized I was pregnant. It would have been easy enough to let Brian have me and pretend it was his. But I couldn't. I told him the truth. And do you know what he said? He said he wanted to marry me and this way he could have me all the quicker. I never even told him who the other man was.'

'The child doesn't know?'

'Nobody knows. You're the first person I've ever told. Brian worships Gloria as though she were his own. And last night I threw it all in his face. I even practically threatened to tell Gloria the truth.'

'It makes no difference. You can't live on gratitude for ever.'

She picked up a cup and held it out, looking steadily at him.

'Oh, but you can, Leonard. That, and what it leads to.'

Brian sat in the cab of his lorry, parked opposite the doors of the school. It was an old building, inadequate for today's needs, with a patched tarmac playground

153

between it and the iron railings along the road. In a couple of years Gloria would leave here for the new secondary modern school set in green fields on the edge of the town. From thinking of this it took no great stretch of the mind to imagine her finished with school and in her first job. The years passed with increasing speed and with every one now she would become less dependent upon him and Joyce and more capable of making her own decisions.

Her birth had been a difficult one and the complications were finally resolved by an operation which made it impossible for Joyce to conceive again. No matter though, that Brian could not have a child of his own; Gloria was as good as his and he loved her fiercely, seeing no necessity for her ever to know the truth about her parentage. It was only Joyce who kept that issue alive, resurrecting it in spasms of fierce and, to him, inexplicable resentment during her attacks of discontent. There was no reason for her to feel gratitude towards him. He had made no sacrifice in marrying her. He'd wanted her and was himself grateful for the circumstances which made her accept him. He doubted that he would have got her otherwise and he had never quite been able to believe his luck. Now he was beginning to wonder if he could hold her. He brooded incessantly on their most recent quarrel and his apparent inability to make her happy.

The doors swung back and the first of the children appeared. He watched for Gloria and got out of the lorry to call her when he saw her.

'Gloria! Over here, love.'

She broke away from her friends and ran to him and he took hold of her and swung her up through the open door of the cab. He climbed in beside her and started the engine.

'Your mummy wants me to take you to her at the shop. You can stop with her till closing time, then she'll take you home.'

'Oh, goody!'

154

The child was used to spending the last part of the afternoon with neighbours, and this visit to the shop was a treat. Brian pondered on the chances of his getting a job with more money so that Joyce could stay at home. And then he wondered whether, even if he doubled his wages, she would ever settle down to the day-to-day routine of the house.

Draper was arranging a stand of ties when they went into the shop.

'Ah, Brian, and little Gloria. Not so little now, though, eh?'

He always addressed him as Brian, but Brian, hesitating at the familiarity of 'Leonard', yet not wishing to be so formal as to call him 'Mr Draper', managed to avoid the use of any name at all.

'Joyce said to bring her round. She said she'd look after her till closing time.'

'Yes, that's all right. Your mummy's gone on a little errand for me, but she won't be long. Come into the inner sanctum.'

'Well, I haven't much time. I'm skyving as it is, you see.'

'You can spare another minute or two, can't you? Don't you want to see Joyce?'

'I suppose I could wait a minute till she comes back.'

'That's right,' Draper said. 'Come through.'

Brian touched Gloria's arm, guiding her ahead of him into the back room where suits hung, shoulder-on, to the wall, and there was a partly unrolled bolt of cloth on the square table.

'I haven't any pop or anything for you to drink,' Draper said. 'Perhaps your mummy will bring you something. I'll tell you what I have got, though.' He reached up and took a box of biscuits off the shelf, opening it and offering it to Gloria. 'I expect you'd like one of these, wouldn't you?'

'Say "thank you",' Brian said as Gloria took a biscuit, and the girl dutifully repeated the words.

Draper patted her on the head. 'That's all right, my

sweet. We don't stand on ceremony here. They're nice, those, aren't they? They're your mummy's favourites as well. Did you know that? I keep telling her she'll spoil her figure but she goes on eating them and it doesn't seem to make any difference. Aren't you glad you've got such a pretty mummy?'

Gloria nodded and said yes.

'And you're going to grow up just as pretty. I can see that. You favour your mummy. Anybody can see whose little girl you are. But I can't see much of your daddy in you.' Draper glanced at Brian as though to confirm his judgement, then looked back at Gloria, his head bent forward and a little to one side as he spoke to her. 'But that's on the right side, isn't it? Your daddy's a big strong man, but you're going to grow up into a pretty lady like your mummy.' Brian frowned as the words brought back once more the pain of his quarrel with Joyce. 'What will you do then? Go on the stage and dance and sing, or act? Your mummy's very good when she's helping me, but she's got your daddy to look after . . .' He stroked her hair once more before looking at Brian.

'I'm afraid I've got nothing to offer you, Brian. Unless you'd like a cup of tea.'

'No, no,' Brian said. 'I shall have to be off.'

'Daddy, can I have a comic?'

'Of course,' Draper said. 'You'll want something to keep you amused while your mummy and I are looking after the shop.' He took a shilling out of his pocket. 'Watch carefully.' He palmed the coin and held out his closed fists to Gloria. 'Which hand do you think it's in?'

'That one.'

'This one?' The hand was empty. 'It must be in the other one, then, mustn't it? No, it's not there, either. I wonder where it can have got to? Do you know? Well, let's try here, shall we?' He put his hand to the side of Gloria's head and pretended to take the shilling out of her ear. 'There it is! Who'd have thought that? Here you are. It's all yours. There's a shop on the corner.'

'Ooh, thank you!' Gloria turned and ran out.

156

'It must be very satisfying to watch a child like that growing and developing as the years go by.' Draper spoke reflectively, his gaze on the open doorway through which Gloria had disappeared. 'Mrs Draper and I never had any children. She wanted to wait. And then she fell ill and died and it was too late. Perhaps she wouldn't have made a good mother. She was a neurotic woman and we weren't happy together. It may sound cruel, but it was a merciful release for me when she died. Some men look for consolation outside their marriage, but I found that sort of thing wasn't enough.'

'Why didn't you get married again?' Brian asked.

'It's not as easy as all that. You're frightened of making another mistake and you don't meet anyone who can overcome that fear in you. Or if you do, perhaps she's already committed elsewhere.'

Brian shrugged as Draper's gaze slid round to his face. He neither liked nor understood him and he was always vaguely uneasy in his company.

'I shall have to be off.'

But Draper came forward in a quick movement before he could leave the room. 'Look, I wanted to tell you. You mustn't be too hard on Joyce, you know.'

'I don't know what you mean.'

'You mustn't judge her too harshly. She was only very young.'

Brian said, 'What're you—?' then stopped as Draper fixed his eyes on something behind him. He turned and saw Gloria was already back and standing in the doorway, a garishly coloured comic in her hands.

'Gloria, just run out for a minute and see if your mummy's coming.'

'Oh, Daddy, I've just been out.'

'Do as you're told.' He watched her go, heard the shop door open and close, then faced Draper. 'Look, tell me what you're talking about.'

Draper's gaze was still fixed in the same direction, holding there so steadily that Brian turned his head again with the momentary thought that Gloria must have

157

deceived him and returned to the doorway. Then he felt the first touch of an inexplicable fear which quickly, as Draper stood motionless, refusing to speak, resolved itself into a conviction that this man knew something which could harm him and the child.

'I want to know what you're talking about,' he said, the edge of his voice roughening.

Draper turned, his head thrust forward as he looked at Brian. As he spoke he moved his hands as though to weave patterns of communication in the air between them. 'It was all over when she met you. I can understand about Brighton, but you mustn't be hard on her. There's nothing between us now.'

Brian stared. Incredulity robbed him for a moment of the power to speak. 'You? You mean . . . you and her?'

'I tell you she was young. It was just one of those things.'

'And Gloria's . . . ?' He couldn't take it in. 'She's not yours,' he said. 'She's mine.'

'How do you think it feels to me?' Draper said. 'Seeing them deprived of things. I could give them a better home and a fuller life.'

'But you can't have them. You can't have either of them.' Something was rising in him, screaming to a point where he could not contain it. He held himself rigid. His body shook and he found that he could discern only the outline of Draper's face as it was thrust at him and the lips moved, letting out words that now had venom in them.

'She's ready to come. She's sick and tired of being grateful to you. Tired of living with you because of what you did for her. How will you stop her if she wants to come? What will you do when she tells you she's leaving?'

'You bas-tard!' The roar of his cry filled the room. He hit Draper in the face, sending him reeling back against the hanging clothes, and sprang after him as he dragged them with him. He took him round the neck and squeezed, his fury uncontainable. 'You'll not have 'em. You'll never take 'em away. They're mine. Mine, I tell you, mine.'

A moment later he realized that he was holding Draper's full weight in his two hands and he let him slip to the floor as Gloria said from the doorway,

'Daddy, what are you doing?'

He ran and crouched and embraced her.

'Daddy, what's wrong?'

'It's all right,' he said. 'He had a dizzy spell. He'll be all right in a minute.' He stood up and took her hand, turning her round. 'We're going for a ride.'

'Aren't we waiting for Mummy?'

'No,' Brian said, 'we're going on a trip.'

Before she could say anything else he swept her up in his arms and carried her out.

He had been driving for some time before he became aware that Gloria was not well. He put his hand on her forehead where she lay curled up, sleeping, on the seat beside him and felt it hot to his touch. Food and a hot drink might help her but he dared not stop at any of the cafés along the road and so mark his route for anyone looking for him. The alarm had probably already been raised. Joyce would be too shocked to cover up for him, even if she wanted to, and the police would quickly discover that he'd been due to call at the shop and now he and Gloria were missing from home.

He had no chance. His flight had been instinctive, an act of panic rather than one containing the possibility of escape. They would get him; but before then he needed somewhere to be quiet for a time, so that he could think. There was only one place he knew.

He drove steadily northwards through lashing rain, his eyes straining to see the road ahead of him. Occasionally he put out his hand and touched the face of the sleeping child, fretting now not about his own predicament but about her having seen what he'd done to

Draper; wondering how much of it she had taken in and how deeply into her mind it had gone.

He woke her to get her out of the lorry but she stood with heavy eyelids, as though drugged, while Mrs Sugden made noises of concern over her head. She appeared to need restful sleep more than food or drink and Mrs Sugden urged him to take her upstairs and put her to bed. There were no questions until he came back down into the kitchen.

'Well?' When he made no answer, Mrs Sugden went on, 'You didn't just bring her for the ride, did you?'

'I've killed him,' Brian said. It had to be like that, quickly, brutally, or he would never have found the courage to tell her.

She caught at her breath, her eyes widening, as Brian moved to the table and pulled out a chair, slumping heavily in to it.

'He taunted me. Said he'd take them away from me and give them a better life than I could. There . . . there was somebody before I met Joyce, y'see. Gloria's his. He said it was him. I suddenly saw him, after all this time, stepping in and taking everything . . . I hit him, then I got hold of him.' Brian turned his hands up on the table. 'I got hold of him. I couldn't think of anything except what he said, what he could do to me.'

There was no need to ask whom he was speaking of. She said, 'Oh, my God!' under her breath and took a bottle of scotch out of the cupboard, pouring some into a glass and handing it to him. He gulped at it, downing it in one, shivering suddenly and pulling a face.

'What're you going to do now?'

He shrugged. 'I don't know. All I could think of was to come here for a bit, somewhere I could be quiet and work something out.'

'But why the little girl? You can't—'

'I just picked her up and brought her with me. I couldn't leave her there with him.'

'You mean to say she saw what happened?'

'Part of it. I don't know how much she really took in.' He lifted his eyes for a moment. 'She's all I've got now.'

'But what are you going to do?'

'I don't know. If I can just rest and be quiet for a while.'

'Do you want something to eat or will you go up to bed?'

He got up and crossed to the fireside chair with the cover over it. 'I'll just put me head down here for a bit.'

She let him be and he slept for a time, waking to find her sitting across from him, very still, her hands in her lap, her gaze in sombre contemplation of his face. For a second it was as though there was nothing out of the ordinary in it; then it all came to him and he said, 'What time is it?'

'It's getting on.'

'Is Gloria all right?'

'Yes. Let her have her sleep out. Does your wife know where you are?'

'I don't suppose so.'

'What will she do?'

'What can she do except call the police? There's nowhere I can go. They'll find me inside twenty-four hours.'

'They can't call it . . . murder, Brian. Not after what he said.'

'Who's to know what he said?'

'You'll have to make 'em believe you. Get her to tell the truth. She's the one who's led you into all this.'

'There you and him, isn't there?' Brian burst out. 'And us in the middle.'

'What do you mean?'

He subsided, unable to carry the thought through. 'I don't know. There's always somebody on to you. They won't leave you alone.'

'You're not without friends, y'know.' She looked at him as he got up without answering. 'D'you hear what I say, Brian?'

He wrested his mind back to her. 'What?'

'You're not on your own.'

'What do you know about it?'

Her gaze wavered then fell. She half-turned her head.

161

It was the first time he had ever seen her outfaced. For the first time it also occurred to him that she might want him. But not simply: in other circumstances she would have contained him in *her* mould, shaped him to *her* design. For his own good.

'I should have thought you'd be glad of anybody who could speak for you,' she said in a moment.

'What could you say?'

'I could tell 'em what sort of man I think you are. I could tell 'em all you've told me about what kind of a dance she's led you.'

'That's your own idea, what *you* think. You never did understand about us.'

She was recovered now and she faced him with the old assurance. 'It doesn't look like it, does it?' she said.

He stood in silence for a time, then shrugged. 'It's no use talking.'

'No. You should be thinking about what you're going to do.'

'There's nothing I can do.'

Whatever Mrs Sugden was going to say then was cut off by the sound from upstairs: a cry that trembled on the edge of becoming a scream.

'That's Gloria' Brian hurried out. A pair of small metal ornaments danced on the mantelshelf as he pounded up the stairs.

Joyce was in the hospital corridor when the trolley came through the double doors. The doctor walking beside the trolley took her arm as she moved forward.

'I've got to talk to him.'

'Are you the one who brought him in?'

'I got the ambulance yes.'

'Are you a relative?'

'No, I work for him. I found him.'

'Do you know what happened?'

'No, that's why I want to talk to him.'

'He's in no state to talk to anybody. He's been very severely manhandled.'

He let her forward sufficiently to lean over the trolley and look at Leonard's face. It was heavily swathed in bandages and the eyes were closed.

'If I waited till he woke up . . .'

'He won't talk to you even then,' the man said. 'His jaw's broken.' He nodded to the porter who pushed the trolley on and into a lift. Joyce turned away as the grille was pulled across. 'Have you spoken to the police?'

'Yes. It wasn't robbery, though. There was nothing missing.'

She had rung the police after calling the ambulance. It was between her putting down the telephone and their arrival a few minutes later that, wondering where Brian and Gloria had got to, she began to connect Brian with what had happened. She telephoned his firm, phrasing her enquiry so that they would have no cause for alarm, and found that he'd not been there since lunchtime.

There was nothing to do now but go home and wait. She had been there for nearly an hour, smoking one cigarette after another in short nervous puffs, her eyes on the television screen but taking in hardly anything, when she remembered that Brian had once written down for her the address and phone number of his lodgings up north.

She found the slip of paper among some letters in the rack on the fireplace and, putting on her coat and counting her loose change, she went out of the house again and walked to the telephone kiosk on the corner.

Brian got Gloria settled in the cab of the lorry, with the help of the rug and the cushion which Mrs Sugden had loaned him, then went back into the house.

'She's all right now she knows she's going home.'

'It's goodbye for a bit, then?' Mrs Sugden said. She grasped his hand. 'You're a good man, Brian. They must see that.'

'I'd better be off,' Brian said. 'If she starts getting upset again . . .'

'You won't forget, will you? What I said about friends.

163

Perhaps it won't be long . . .' She reached up and kissed him on the mouth then let go of his hand and turned away.

She heard the door close behind him and the engine start. She had gone out and was watching the tail lights of the vehicle moving away along the road when the telephone began to ring in the hall.

'I thought I'd killed him.'

He had said it before, in the same slow disbelieving way, and the stupid wonderment of it angered her.

'You bloody fool, Brian, for believing what he said.'

'It wasn't true, was it?'

'Of course it wasn't true. I've told you it wasn't.'

'Why should he say a thing like that? Why should he make it up?'

'How do I know? To cause trouble. Because he's evil-minded. He made a pass at me, said he wanted me. When I turned him down all he could think of was making trouble.'

'And I thought I'd killed him.'

'You didn't even get that right, did you? Taking Gloria and running away like that, and all for nothing. You're a fool, Brian, a bloody useless fool.'

'Don't keep saying that, you selfish bitch. I spent nearly twelve hours, thinking he was dead; thinking I'd have to do ten years for him. And all you can say is "you bloody fool". Well, you're right: I am a fool, a fool for putting up with your rotten, selfish ways. I did it for her. It was her I was thinking about. If I thought I could keep her he could have you tomorrow.'

'Who the hell do you think you are, talking to me like that?'

He reached out and took her by the wrist, dragging her to her feet. 'I know who I am, and you'll listen when I talk – bitch.'

It was the first time he had ever laid a finger on her in anger and for a moment the shock of it took her voice.

'God! I hate you, you big useless—'

'And I hate you, so what are you going to do about it?'

She swung her free arm, aiming to strike him across the face, but he caught that wrist too and held her there in the grip of both his hands. The glare of outrage in her eyes was akin to that of desire. She was beautiful in her anger. He knew that to bear her down and take her now, on the floor, quickly and without tenderness, would be a greater satisfaction to him than striking her, and a more searing humiliation to her.

The moment held. She stared him out, defying him to do what he liked. Another thought slid into his mind and was expressed before he could decide its wisdom.

'Do you ever think about him?' Brian asked. 'The one who did give you the kid?'

Her eyes narrowed as though she did not instantly understand. Then, 'Yes,' she said. She threw her head back as she saw his face, and screamed. 'Yes. Bloody yes!'

He pushed her away from him on to the sofa and went across to where he had left his donkey jacket on a chair. She watched him put it on.

'Where are you going?'

'I'm taking the lorry back to the yard and leaving a note for the boss.'

'Will you want anything to eat when you come back?'

'No.'

'Are you going to work today?'

'No.'

'What are we going to do?'

'What about?'

'Us.'

'What do you want to do?'

'Go on living.'

'That's all we can do, isn't it?'

He went out, closing the inner door after him. She stared for a long time at the fire and then went upstairs and brought down her clothes, turning on the radio before she left the room. She had undressed once she had known he was on his way back. Now she slowly

165

began to dress again, uncovering and reclothing one part of her body at a time as a voice read the early morning news bulletin . . .

'. . . Miss Forrest is one of the most sought-after stars in the film world today. Travelling with Miss Forrest was her husband, Mr Ralph D. Packenheimer, whose business interests in the United States include motels and drive-in cinemas. They were married a month ago and London is their last stop on a round-the-world honeymoon tour which has taken in seven countries. Mr Packenheimer is Miss Forrest's fourth husband.

'Arriving on the same flight at London Airport was the Prime Minister of the newly independent African state of Kandaria, Mr Walter Umbala, who is here on an unofficial visit. Our reporter asked Mr Umbala about recent unrest and disturbances in Kandaria. He said that in a nation of mixed races and religions there were bound to be disagreements from time to time, but they only became serious when exploited by outside agencies for their own ends. "We must be ever vigilant and resist these outside elements with all our might," Mr Umbala said. "Only then shall we go forward, united and strong, to our destiny among the free nations of the world—" '

Joyce gave a small exclamation of impatience and turned the tuner till she found some music. She lit a cigarette and sat down, looking at the fire and hearing under the sound of the wireless the soft shift of the hot coals, as she waited for Brian to come back.

This Day, Then Tomorrow

Something out of the ordinary had happened in the Hatton household. Ruth, at twenty-two the youngest of the Hatton girls, had got a novel accepted for publication. The publisher's letter was on the breakfast table when she came down, and the sudden joyful spring of colour to her cheeks as she opened and read it betrayed her to Mrs Hatton, so that she was forced to break the news not at a moment of her own choosing, but there and then.

'£250 advance on royalties!' Mrs Hatton said. 'And what's this novel about, ever?'

Ruth made a movement of her hand. 'Oh ...'

'£250?' Mr Hatton took the letter in his turn. 'I didn't know you were writing a novel, Ruth.'

'She's been going to that literature class in the evenings for nearly two years,' Mrs Hatton said, as though he were somehow more remiss than herself in not knowing what their daughter was up to. 'And she's always scribbled in her room.'

'I thought she was studying people like Shakespeare and Dickens,' Mr Hatton said, 'not writing books of her own.'

'Why ever shouldn't Ruth write a novel, Bernard?' Mrs Hatton said. 'She's had a good education.'

Mr Hatton was too used to his wife's instant allotting of their roles in any situation – her own one of perception and concern, his that of a neglectful obtuseness – to become irritated.

'We study literary composition,' Ruth said, 'and we're expected to do some original writing.'

'But a novel!' Ruth's older sister Celia said. 'You can't deny you've kept it quiet, Ruth. It must have made a fair-sized parcel to put in the post.'

'Well . . . I didn't know whether it was any good or not, so there was no point in saying anything yet.'

'But we're here to share your disappointments as well as your successes, surely, Ruth,' her mother said.

Some of them, anyway, Ruth thought. She had prepared herself for their knowing if the manuscript were returned, but she could not have endured the initial waiting period except alone. Once her mother had seized on such an event outside the normal life of the household she would not have let it drop. There would also have been the necessity of letting her read and comment on the book. Now, of course, when it had acquired a *cachet* of a publisher's acceptance, it was different. Or was it? The contents were still the same, and soon now they would become public property. For the first time Ruth felt a tiny tremor of anxiety.

Her father was more concerned with the business aspects of the matter.'They say they'll send you a contract to sign,' he said. 'Perhaps you ought to get legal advice on that.'

'It's a standard procedure.'

'Yes, but you don't want to sign your rights away.'

'Dad, they're among the most reputable publishers in London.'

'You don't think they're going to cheat the girl, do you, Bernard?' Mrs Hatton said.

'Of course not. But they're businessmen and it's their job to make a profit.'

'Perhaps you can let Mr Astley glance at it, Ruth,' her mother suggested.

Mr Astley had acted for Mr Hatton in the purchase of their house and in a number of other routine matters. Ruth didn't think that he, or any other solicitor in the district, would know much about authors' rights in a literary agreement.

'I'll show it to my tutor at the class,' she said. 'He's

had poetry published, and some stories.'

Mrs Hatton's mouth pursed in an expression that was almost a smirk. 'What a feather in your cap when you walk in and tell them about it!'

Mr Hatton, leaving first, patted Ruth's head and twinkled at her from the doorway. 'Well done! It looks as though we're going to have a celebrity in the house.'

She was called to the telephone in her free period that morning. The male voice at the other end of the line belonged to a reporter on the local weekly newspaper.

'I understand you've had a novel accepted for publication.'

'Well, yes. How do you know?'

'Your mother rang the editor, I believe.'

Ruth felt a spasm of irritation. She had wanted to savour the good news privately for a while; to ponder this development in her life and come to terms with it before speaking of it to anyone. But already she was being pushed along at someone else's pace.

'I wondered if I could come along and talk to you about it. It'll make a very interesting item for our readers.'

'Our readers.' Everybody. Common knowledge. That Hatton girl's written a book. She suddenly became acutely conscious of how many people who didn't read a novel from one year's end to the next would read this one because she was its author. And how, of course, they would presume to judge it. With that thought came a keen desire to put this man off, to make any excuse to avoid having to talk to him. But wasn't all this part of the process? She had written a book and offered it for publication. So now the public would read it, and what they made of it and her were factors over which she had little control. She ought to be flattered and pleased by this instant opportunity of publicity, but instead she felt something more like fright. Oh, Lord! Why had she done it?

'Well, then?' she asked.

'I thought I might call round this evening. We go to press tomorrow.'

'But it'll be months before the book's published.'

'Oh, we can do a follow-up piece nearer the time, but we'd like to be first with the original story.'

First among whom? Who else could be interested?

She said, 'All right. Will seven o'clock be convenient?'

'Righto, seven. I have the address.'

Arthur Debenham, who taught Senior English, passed by as she left the telephone cubicle. He glanced at her and nodded. Ruth turned her head and watched him stroll along the corridor with his long slow stride and curious swing of the shoulders. Debenham was in his fifties and given to occasional caustic denunciations in the staff room of contemporary trends in the arts. What usually provoked him were newspaper reports of a new play or novel by 'the latest back-street genius from Bradford' or 'Bermondsey'. 'We're living in the age of the literate illiterate,' was Debenham's line. Everybody's writing novels or plays. They've none of them anything to say, and they don't know how to say it anyway, but they're so full of their own insignificant – and usually grubby – feelings, they have to share them with the world.'

What would he make of her adding to the number? Because soon he would know. Everybody would know.

'A few biographical details first, I think.' The reporter was a young man about Ruth's age. It was raining outside and his gingerish suede boots were darkly wet on the toes, but he had gauchely declined to remove the blue anorak which he wore over a grey roll-neck sweater and Mrs Hatton glanced at him from time to time as though apprehensive that he would lean back and stain with damp the lime-green cover of the chair in which he was sitting. But he remained forward on the edge, a cheap throwaway ballpoint poised over the open notebook on his knee. Beside him on the arm of the chair the cup of tea Mrs Hatton had pressed upon him stood untouched and cooling, with a biscuit soggily absorbing the liquid slopped over into the saucer.

'You're, er, how old?'

'Twenty-two.'

'You were educated at the local grammar school?'

'Yes.'

'And then . . . ?'

'I went to a training college.'

'And now you teach, what, domestic science? Why didn't you study a subject connected with writing?'

'I've always been interested in housecraft and so on. The writing thing's comparatively recent.'

'Even as a little girl Ruth was handy about the house,'Mrs Hatton put in. 'Of course I encouraged her and taught her all I could, purely for the sake of it. That kind of ability's never lost.'

'No, quite . . . So how did you become interested in writing?'

'I started going to a literary composition class in the evenings, just as a change. We were expected to do some writing of our own.'

'How long did it take you to write this novel?'

'Oh, about a year.'

'That would be working in the evenings?'

'And a few hours at weekends, when I could manage.'

'Did your family encourage you?'

'They didn't know what I was doing.'

'Oh?' The young man looked at Mrs Hatton, who tried an indulgent laugh.

'No, we had no idea until this morning when the letter came.'

'You preferred nobody to know?'

'Well, yes. I think when you've never done anything like that before it seems a very personal thing. You become rather self-conscious about it. I mean, it might just be self-indulgence.'

'But in your case, it seems the novel is good enough for publication.'

'Yes. Perhaps I've been lucky.'

'I think you're too modest, Miss Hatton. Publishers have their standards.'

'I think so too,' her mother said. 'We're all very proud of her.'

'By the way, what's the book called?'

'*This Day, then Tomorrow.*'

The reporter repeated the title after her, putting it in full among the shorthand symbols in his notebook.

'And can you give me some idea of what it's about?'

She had expected that question, and thought about it at odd moments in the day, but without much result.

'Well . . . that's not easy.'

'I don't expect you to tell me the plot. But is it a love story, a thriller, or an historical piece . . . you know.'

'It hasn't got much of a plot to tell. It's a love story, I suppose.' Oh yes, it was about love. And innocence. About the necessity for trust and the inevitability of its defencelessness in the face of betrayal.

'A romantic novel.'

'Oh no. It doesn't fall into that slot.'

The firmness of her reply quickened his interest. 'You mean it's too outspoken?'

'I'd prefer to say it's honest.'

'What about the main characters, and the background?'

'The main character is a girl who's away from home for the first time, at college.'

'You mean, like yourself?'

'No, not exactly.'

'It's not autobiographical, then?'

'No, look. A writer uses settings and the kind of life he or she knows well then adds observation and imagination.'

'I see. So you don't expect the reader to identify you with the main character.'

'I hope not. If you'd read the book I don't think you'd ask me that.'

'Oh, why not?'

'The girl in the novel has an abortion.'

And now she had gone too far, revealed much more than at this stage she had ever intended. Her mother's gaze was on her. Did it contain the first flicker of alarm?

Ruth said quickly, 'Look, I'd be grateful if you didn't mention that. It sounds so sensational out of context.'

'Well, of course not, if you say so.' The reporter looked disappointed at losing the spicy core of his story as soon as it had been revealed. 'But our readers aren't going to be shocked by the mention of a word like that.'

'I know your readers,' Ruth said. 'They've got the same proportion of the prudish, the hypocritical, the bigoted, and the just plain ignorant as any other community, and I don't think it's fair that either I or my book should be prejudged by mentioning such an emotive subject at this stage. I can justify what I've written in its context, but they'll have to read the book to arrive at a balanced judgement.'

'I think you could be wrong.' The young man frowned. 'A little bit of the right kind of publicity can help to sell books.'

'That's not the kind of publicity I want.'

'Certainly not,' Mrs Hatton said. 'We do have to live in this town.'

'Yes, of course. But . . .' Ruth could almost hear him thinking: But if that's the case you can't blame me if your daughter writes a book which she finds it embarrassing to talk about.

She began to bring the interview to a close.

'Have you got as much as you need to be going on with?'

'Yes, I suppose so. Just a few more background facts. Your father is Mr Hatton the dentist? And have you any brothers or sisters?'

'Ruth has an older sister who works for a firm of estate agents,' Mrs Hatton said, 'and my eldest daughter is married to an officer in the army, who's stationed abroad at present.'

'Righto, then. Thank you very much.' The young man stood up, almost dislodging with his elbow the tea-cup beside him. 'Sorry, I'd forgotten that.' He took the cup and in his eagerness to show that he'd really wanted the tea, drank the lot so quickly that drops spilled down the front of his anorak. The biscuit, he left in the saucer.

'It will be in the paper this weekend?' Mrs Hatton asked.

'All being well. By the way, do you know when the book's being published?'

'I've no idea.' Ruth gave a little laugh. 'It's all a bit premature, really. I haven't even signed the contract yet.'

'Oh, that'll be all right, I'm sure,' the young man said. 'I'll look forward to reading it.'

She saw him out then went back into the sitting-room. Her mother was standing on the hearthrug.

'Don't you think it's time you let me read this book?'

'If you want to.'

'Well, of course I want to. I want to for its own sake; and after this weekend people are bound to stop me and mention it. I ought to know what my daughter's been doing, didn't I?'

Ruth said, 'I'll get it for you now.' She went to her room and brought down the carbon of the typescript. Her mother felt the weight.

'There seems to be a lot of it.'

'It'll be a normal-length book when it gets into print.'

'It's not the kind of thing you can read in bed, anyway. All that typing, and I never knew.'

'The typing's the least of it,' Ruth said. 'By the time you reach the final copy you're laughing.'

Mrs Hatton glanced at the first couple of pages. 'Ruth . . . it isn't . . . well, sensational, is it? I mean, there's so much stuff between covers these days that I wouldn't have in the house.'

'I've written a novel, Mother,' Ruth said. 'It's neither a fairy story nor something that exploits dirt for its own sake or for money. You'll have to make up your own mind.'

The young reporter rang up the next morning to ask for a photograph of Ruth. Mrs Hatton lent him a formal portrait taken while Ruth was at college. Ruth didn't like it. She wasn't unattractive, she knew. She had been told more than once that her legs were good and there had been a time when she would stop on catching sight of her naked body in a mirror and take in the fineness of her skin and the way her narrow back emphasized the plumpness of her breasts in a sensual reverie of self-love which was a reflection of another's professed adoration, an exulting in what she had to give and the way in which it was taken. Once upon a time . . . But all the camera ever showed was a pale bespectacled face with an insipid half-smile: the face of one fitted for nothing more passionate than studying, passing examinations, writing a book. There was, she supposed wryly, a kind of justice in it.

Her mother read the manuscript during the day, when she was alone in the house. Ruth found herself tensed for the reaction and tried to interpret something from her mother's behaviour. But there was nothing to be seen and no word passed between them on the subject until Mrs Hatton had finished the novel.

'I suppose it's well written. I don't know what other people will make of it, though.' Ruth was silent. 'It's not . . . well, it's hardly the kind of book I'd have expected you to write.'

'Oh?'

'Did you . . . did you know somebody at college who had an abortion?'

'You pick up all manner of information if you keep your eyes and ears open, if you talk to people, listen to what they tell you, and fill in the bits they don't.'

'But this girl that the book's about, who has the love affair. Was it necessary to go into so much detail?'

'I wanted to make it vivid and real.'

'Yes, but . . . I must say, I felt myself blushing more than once. Why, there are things in there I hardly knew about myself.'

'Oh, come on, Mother. You've had three children.'

'Well, I didn't know till after I was married.'

'Times change.'

'Yes. So I'm to take it – I mean, I can't do any other than take it – that you've already—'

'Mother,' Ruth said firmly, 'the book's the book and my private life is my own business.'

'All the same, when I think of the mortal danger you've been in. And I thought I'd brought you up so well, the three of you.'

'I'm sorry, Mother, but if you call bringing-up well teaching your daughters to bake and sew, seeing they're fed and clothed, encouraging them to go to church once a week, but telling them almost nothing about some of the most fundamental aspects of life, then you can't wonder they expose themselves to mortal danger the minute they leave the house.'

'Well, if that's what you think . . .'

'I'm sorry, Mother, really,' Ruth said. 'I didn't mean to hurt you.'

The words had, indeed, sounded shockingly harsh; but she was on the defensive, fearful of an attitude which could sap her confidence, turn her pride in something honestly achieved into a timid conformity with all those stultifying approaches to life that she most detested.

'I'm sorry if you think I've failed you in any way,' her mother said stiffly.

'Just so long as—' Ruth began, then stopped.

'So long as what?'

So long as you don't cripple me now by imposing your small-town sensibility on me, was that she wanted to say. But that would only force her mother further into injured pride.

'Mother, I know,' she said carefully, 'that I'm bound to come up against a number of people who'll put the worst possible construction on what I've done. But I hope they'll be far out-numbered by the other people who'll like and appreciate the book, or at least respect it for what it's meant to be. I want to think you're one of the latter people and that you're on my side.'

'I'm always on your side, you know that, whatever you

do and I shall defend you to the last. I just can't help wishing you'd written, well, a *nicer* book, something more wholesome. I don't know what your father will make of it, I'm sure.'

'Doesn't it affect you at all?' Ruth said. 'Don't you find yourself concerned for the girl in any way?'

'Oh, yes, I'm sorry for her. All that sorrow and pain. And there's no doubt that the young man does treat her shabbily. But on the other hand, I can't help feeling that most of it's her own fault. And as for that awful mother, always putting her husband down . . .'

Ruth began to smile but her mother, not looking at her didn't see. There was a silence, then Mrs Hatton sighed.

'I suppose it'll be all right in the long term.'

'A nine-day wonder,' Ruth said.

'All the same, I'm rather sorry now I was in such a hurry to ring up the paper. I could have had a little time to get used to it all if I'd read the book first.'

Ruth laughed.

'Never mind. Let's hope it makes a lot of money for me. That'll justify it in everybody's eyes.'

But oh, that damned self-consciousness!

It started at the beginning of her first class on Monday morning, with whispers in a group of junior-school girls.

'Saw your picture in the paper, Miss.'

'Have you really wrote a book, Miss?'

'Written,' Ruth corrected. 'Written a book.'

'Well, have you, Miss?'

'Yes, I have.'

'What's it about, Miss?'

'Are you going to be on the telly, Miss?'

'Now, look, let's all settle down, shall we? This isn't the time to go into all that. This morning we're going to make some biscuits . . .'

She met Arthur Debenham drinking coffee in the staff room during morning break.

'Ah, here's our own Edna O'Drabble. Or is it Margaret Brien?'

'What a lot of ignorance you pretend to, Arthur,' Ruth said. 'Have you really not read either of them?'

'You ought to know by now, Ruth, that only the literary dead have any chance of winning Arthur's grudging respect,' Lois Rayner said. 'His secret vice is lesser known women novelists of the Edwardian period.'

Ruth laughed. Lois was a toughie; a stocky, flat-chested spinster of about Debenham's age, with yellow in the roots of her grey hair and ferocious flyaway frames on her glasses.

'No, I wanted to congratulate you,' Debenham said. 'I suppose it's still something of an achievement to get a book published, even in these days. Perhaps it's expecting too much to hope that it might be readable as well.'

Ruth gasped and flushed heavily as he put down his cup and walked away. Even Lois was taken aback.

'Of all the miserable devils!' she said as the door closed behind him.

'I don't suppose he meant it to be taken like that,' Ruth said.

'If he knows so much about English Literature he should have learned how to frame his words at his age.' Lois's eyes flashed behind her glasses. She poured coffee and handed Ruth a cup. 'Here you are, honey. I think you'll learn more about stupidity than malice. Though they do say the literary world's riddled with it. That and back-scratching. You do my washing and I'll do yours.'

'I wouldn't know about that. I'm just a novice.'

'First steps,' Lois said. 'Who knows what they can lead to? Anyway, I hope you'll give me a signed copy for sticking up for you.'

Ruth smiled. 'I'll see what I can do.'

'They do say his wife gives him hell.'

'Oh?'

'Oh, yes. Makes his life a misery, by all accounts.'

From the members of the evening class she received an envy in which she basked, behind an outward demeanour that was quietly modest. The class met in an adult-education centre in a larger town some miles from Ruth's home, and the first some of her fellow students knew of her success was when their tutor, Jim Thomas, announced it at the start of the session.

'Our congratulations are due to Ruth Hatton, who's got a novel accepted for publication. And our admiration for her reticence in keeping the fact that she was working on one to herself until it was proved successful.'

Thomas shared the envy of the others. 'D'you know I've written three novels without one offer of publication?' he said to her afterwards.

'But you've published poems and stories.'

'Yes, just enough to reassure me that I'm not wasting my time entirely.'

'Oh, come now. I don't know how you can talk like that.'

'Don't you? It's one thing spouting in a knowledgeable way about the subject, and another doing it oneself.'

'But isn't there an awful lot of stuff published that you wouldn't put your name to?'

'Oh, yes. And quite a bit I'd give my eye teeth to have written.'

'Well, you don't know yet which category my book comes into.'

'No, that's true.' He looked at her reflectively for a second, then they laughed together.

'And now I shall be terribly self-conscious about your seeing it.'

'You won't have any choice, though. If you offer something to the world, the world has a right to express its opinion.'

'Yes.'

'Does the thought bother you?'

'A little.'

'The excitement must more than make up for it, though, eh?'

'Oh, yes!'

The sudden clear blaze of delight in her eyes made

him laugh out loud again. He put his hand on her shoulder as they walked to the door.

'I wish you luck with it.'

An antidote to Mrs Hatton's reaction, and the largely uncomprehending wonder of the family's friends and acquaintances, was provided by a trip to London to see the publishers. Half-term was fortunately near so Ruth was able to arrange to go within ten days of their asking to see her.

London was hot, the air heavy. After a short journey on the Underground she took a wrong turning and for a time was lost. When she rediscovered her direction she was late and had to hurry, arriving at the tall old house in a leafy square, near the British Museum, with the composure she had gradually drawn round herself on the train evaporated in the heat, and feeling her body sticky inside the suit which had seemed just right in the chilly morning at home, but which was far too heavy for the weather here.

Ruth had imagined vaguely, in her naivety, a place like a newspaper building, with glass-partitioned offices and the faint hum of printing presses from below; but here she was reminded of a solicitor's premises as, after waiting in the reception office for a few minutes, she was led up the narrow creaking stairs past the blank doors on each landing.

The room she was shown into had two tall paned windows looking out on to the green foliage of the trees. It had obviously been an upstairs drawing-room when, in the time of a novelist like Thackeray, the houses in the square were occupied by London's prosperous upper middle class. She wondered how many distinguished literary figures of today had been shown into this room, offered a seat in this overstuffed armchair of indeterminate age, and plied with cigarettes and sherry, as she was now while polite enquiries were made about her journey and small talk exchanged about London and the unexpected warm weather. The cigarette she refused, the sherry she accepted. The diversion of an incoming telephone call allowed her a few moments to turn her head to the books on the fronted shelves behind her: row after row of the firm's titles at which she peered to see the names of those writers published under the imprint to which she herself would soon belong.

'Well . . .' Raymond Waterford put down the receiver and smiled at her across his desk. He was the firm's editorial director, the person with whom she had corresponded, a bulky man in his middle forties with untidy thinning wavy hair and a square fleshy face. He wore a navy-blue pinstriped suit and, in flamboyant contrast, a huge yellow bow tie with blue spots. He fiddled with a new briar pipe but didn't fill it. He wasn't a pipe-smoker, he'd already told her, but he was trying any method he could think of to break himself of the habit of an enormous daily consumption of cigarettes.

'We like your novel very much, Miss Hatton. All my colleagues agree with me about its exceptional quality.'

'Thank you.'

'It isn't always the case. Are you working on something else?'

'I haven't had the time since I finished that one.'

'You mean we're the first people to see it?'

'Yes.'

'What made you choose us?'

'You publish one or two writers I admire. If you're good enough for them you should be all right for me.'

Waterford laughed. 'Quite. And I think you'll find we're as good as anyone else in London at selling fiction. You are going to write another novel, though, I take it?'

'Oh, yes. I'm mulling over an idea now.'

'Good. A publisher likes to look to the future, you know. Most first novels don't make any money; it's with the second or third that the dividends start to come in. In this case, though, providing the reviewers can see what's in front of their noses, and the public respond in the right way, we might have a small success. But don't let me build you up too much. This business is full of people who've come unstuck with their predictions.'

Ruth hesitated. It seems silly here in this room. But she asked just the same.

'You don't think it might be a bit too much in parts?'

'What? How d'you mean?'

'A bit outspoken.'

'Too graphic, d'you mean? Goodness me, no. Nobody here has suggested anything of the kind.' He smiled. 'Do you still live with your family?' Ruth nodded. 'I sometimes think,' he said 'that the only tenable situation for a writer would be an omniscient anonymity, knowing everything but not taking any part in it.'

'You mean something like a Catholic priest?'

He gave a guffaw. 'Yes, something like that.'

'Except that readers seem inclined to see it the other way round,' Ruth said. 'That it's the writer who's making the confession.'

'Yes . . .' His attention had wandered. He moved papers on his desk as though looking for something, then glanced at his watch. 'We ought to be going to lunch.'

He asked if she wanted to freshen up and, calling in the girl who had brought her upstairs, had Ruth shown to a small lavatory on the next landing. Then, a few minutes later, she and Waterford were walking across the square, he swinging a tightly rolled umbrella with which he pointed the way at each intersection. In the restaurant, a low-ceilinged room with oak-panelled walls, red velvet upholstery and quiet, attentive waiters who addressed Waterford by name, Ruth, her tongue loosened by a mixture of excitement and wine, became talkative, telling Waterford at his prompting, about her family, her career at college, her work now, and which writers she admired. At one point she recognized the face of an actor whom she'd seen in films at a nearby table and Waterford amused her by recounting a slightly scandalous anecdote about the man. Then Ruth switched to questioning him. When was her book likely to be published? How long before she would see the proofs . . . ?

'You haven't got an agent, have you?' Waterford asked.

'No. Should I have?'

'Yes. You won't be able to handle the subsidiary rights yourself. A paperback sale is our province, but then there are all the other pickings: foreign rights, both in the United States and on the Continent; possible serialization before publication; film rights, and so on.'

'Can you recommend anybody?'

'I should think so. It's a question of who'll be best for you. How long are you going to be in town?'

'Till tomorrow. I'm staying with a friend tonight.'

'In any case, he'd want to read the book before deciding whether or not to take you on. Have you got a spare typescript?'

'Just one carbon.'

'If you could send that on to me as soon as you get back. You won't need it, will you?'

'I don't suppose so.'

'No. You forget this one now and get on with the next. In any case, if I have it you've a perfect excuse for preventing people from reading it before the proofs are ready.' He smiled.

'All right.'

'I fancy it's something that writers have to get used to,' he said, returning to the subject they'd begun to discuss in his office. 'I mean the question of saying in print what you possibly wouldn't discuss in so-called polite society. It's not easy to be honest. So far as I can gather the solution is to find an environment in which you can feel free and at ease, yet not cut off altogether from the sources of your inspiration – if we may use such a word. Your material, if you like. That's why so many young writers come to London after their first success. And why too many of them find that in doing so they've lost their basic nourishment. The other side of the coin is the danger in becoming too big a fish in too small a pond.'

'The pond may be small,' Ruth said. 'But I think it's very deep.'

'Well, then. We shall have to wait and see what you haul out of it with your next book. In the meantime, you won't really mind becoming quite well known and having your picture in the papers, will you?'

'No,' Ruth admitted. 'No, I don't suppose I shall.'

'No,' Waterford said, 'you'd be quite a rare human being if you did.'

In the middle of the afternoon, slightly muzzy headed from the lunchtime wine, Ruth made her way by Underground to the flat of her friend, in Baron's Court. Monica Darrell had been in Ruth's year at college, but soon after qualifying she had given up teaching to go on the stage. After a year with a provincial repertory company she had landed a regular role in a television serial and now she was combining this with a part in a long-running West End play, which had been recast for the second time.

'I wish you'd write something decent for me,' Monica said. 'This play I'm in is a terribly creaky old thing; but the public love it and it looks as though it'll run forever. Why don't you write a super television play and tell them you simply must have me for the lead?'

'I'll have to think about that,' Ruth said.

'It's all a living, though. And God knows I shouldn't grumble when there are any number like me out of work. Anyway, it's lovely to see you, Ruth, and absolutely marvellous news about the novel. You are a sly boots, though, not saying anything about it before.'

Ruth gave the excuse she'd given everyone else. Not that she minded one bit Monica's reading the book. She was the kind of intelligent equal for whom she'd written it, and whom she expected to be her most perceptive audience.

'When is it coming out, then?'

'They're going to try to get it into the autumn list. That means before Christmas at the latest.'

'And do they seem pleased with it?'

'Yes, they were very flattering.'

'Let's hope you have a big success with it, get lovely notices and make pots of money.'

Ruth turned from the window. They were high up under the roof of the house. 'That field's a bit of luck, isn't it?' she said. 'So totally unexpected when you're in the street.'

'It's the grounds of a church,' Monica told her. 'You can't see the building itself for those trees, but if you look past that wall you can just make out the tops of some gravestones.'

Ruth sat down on the bed-settee. 'You know,' she said. 'I've got the funniest feeling about the book. I think it's going to do very well indeed.' She was silent for a moment, then she laughed, breaking the intent seriousness of her features. 'Probably no more than wishful thinking.'

'Sillier things have happened, as my Aunt Amelia used to say. You just keep your fingers crossed, lovey, and hope for the best.'

Monica brewed a pot of tea and made some toast.

'Lucky I'm written out of the series for a couple of weeks,' she said, 'or I should hardly have had a chance to talk to you. When I'm rehearsing that and doing the play as well it's all go, go, go from nine-thirty in the morning till ten-thirty at night. I usually wait and eat properly after the show. Then if I'm lucky there's someone to pay for my supper too.'

'Is there anybody special?'

'No, not just now. And that reminds me.' Monica arrested the motion of the teacup towards her mouth. 'I saw Maurice Waring the other week.'

'Oh? Where?'

'In the Salisbury. I nipped in for a drink with a friend after the show and there he was.'

'Did you speak to him?'

'For a minute. He seemed quite pleased to see me. Glamour of the stage, and all that. I suppose he'll be mad keen to read your book when he hears about it. Very fond of the off-beat success things, is our Maurice.'

'Did he say what he was doing now?'

'Teaching at a grammar school somewhere in the Home Counties. I forget just where he said. Ruth, he's not queer at all, is he?'

'Whatever makes you ask that?'

'Oh, I don't know exactly. Something about the way he was standing there eyeing people when we went in. Maybe my imagination. He was probably just looking out for celebrities.'

'Anyway,' Ruth said, 'I don't know that he is. Or I should say was.'

'You should know, I suppose,' Monica's gaze lingered on her for a second. Ruth felt it rather than saw, because stupidly she couldn't bring herself at this moment to look back at Monica. She had nothing to hide. Except, that was, the way her heart had lurched at the mention of his name, and the trembling hollowness just under her ribs now, which it seemed to her must show in an unsteady control of her voice.

'Is he married, or anything?'

'How can he be if I got the impression he might be queer? But then, I don't know. I didn't ask him and he didn't say.'

'Did he . . . did he ask about me?' She was impatient with herself for putting the question. She had thought herself in command of her emotions on the subject; that the long labour of the novel had purged her of bitterness, bringing her to the realization that to keep her wounds open was to destroy the beauty of what she had felt at the time. She had come to terms with it, so she'd thought. But now she was undone again, jealous of Monica who had spoken to him, stood near him, only a few weeks ago, when she herself had not seen him for more than two years.

'He asked about the old gang in general, then mentioned you. Did I ever see you. So I told him we wrote to each other, and what you were doing.'

'And that was that?'

'Yes. What else did you expect?'

'Nothing.'

'Ruth . . .' Monica said in a moment, gently chiding.

'I know.' Ruth poured herself another cup of tea. 'He'll get a shock if he does read the novel.'

'Oh? It's all in there, is it?'

'Well, I used it rather than recorded it. I mean, that's what a writer does. But it's close enough for him to recognize it. The girl in the book has an abortion.'

'Wow! You don't mean . . . ? You couldn't have . . .'

'Not without you and perhaps some of the others knowing, no. But he'd gone away by that time. No, I just extended it all a bit, pushed it to a further extreme. I did think for a time that I was pregnant, you see.'

'And you never said a word!'

'No, I kept it to myself. Terrified out of my wits for nearly three weeks.'

'I don't think I was ever absolutely certain that you and he . . .'

'Had been sleeping together? Weren't you? It was bloody marvellous, Monica. The most stupendous up-lifting experience of my life. Until it turned sour, of course.'

'I was never quite sure before how badly he'd behaved . . . So when he reads the novel he's going to wonder if you . . .'

'I expect he will.'

'Serve the swine right. If he's got enough conscience for it. Of course, I've got to be honest and tell you that I never really did care for him myself . . .'

In the early evening they set out for the theatre. While Monica was getting ready for the performance, Ruth wandered along Shaftesbury Avenue, looking into the shop windows. The play was, as Monica had said, a rather creaky, contrived piece and not the kind of thing she would have gone to on her own initiative. But Ruth had never seen her friend working on the stage before and was glad of the chance. Afterwards, she met Monica at the stage door.

'Is there anywhere special you'd like to go?'

'I don't think I've ever been to that pub you mentioned. The Salisbury, was it?'

'Oh, it's just a place in St Martin's Lane where you can sometimes find a few actors after the show.' Monica paused.

'It's not his local, you know, Ruth.'

'No,' Ruth said. She felt foolish, found out in something unworthy of her. 'Let's go and eat, shall we?'

While still in London she could to some extent keep her main concerns at bay; but once on the train, with the thread which connected her to the familiar and the past drawing tighter over every mile, she gave herself to a brooding examination of her state of mind.

The conviction which had come to her yesterday, that the novel would be a success, was as strong as ever; and on its foundation she allowed herself to build the notion of a new life. She saw opening out before her prospects of which she would hitherto hardly have dreamed; saw them with a prophetic clarity, but soberly now, without elation. For she knew that whatever small measures of fame and fortune came to her with this book would have to be justified by the long and continuous labour of the future; saw also that the task before her would provide no magic shield against the disappointments and deprivations of her life; rather would it, in its conscientious execution, expose her to a raw-nerved apprehension of reality such as she had never known before.

And, oh, that all this should have come to her so soon, while the joy was still fresh in her!

If she were not, therefore, to lose everything there was above all else the grave necessity of making something of *herself*: of learning somehow to hang on until she found, if not happiness, a strength of mind to endure whatever in its probing, analysis and self-questioning this new life could challenge her with, so that through it all she would in her basic purpose keep firm and true both to her talent and the memory of that exultant

188

womanhood she had known when Maurice loved her.

Had she been a praying girl she would have prayed. As it was, she closed her eyes and addressed herself with stern resolve.

A little while later a white-jacketed steward slid open the door of the compartment and announced the first sitting for lunch. Ruth had not thought herself hungry but now she got up and made her way towards the dining-car, swaying from side to side as she balanced herself against the motion of the train.

THE END

Just You Wait and See
Stan Barstow

'Mr Barstow's strength is in the resolute honesty of his
depiction of how people feel. He is a writer you can trust'
THE SCOTSMAN

Set in a closely-knit industrial community at the beginning
of the Second World War, Stan Barstow's novel tells the
story of young Ella Palmer and her family. Ella wants to
marry, but her affections are torn between the solid,
dependable qualities of Walter, a local butcher, and the
romantic enticements of Mr Strickland, a visiting
tradesman with knowledge of the world beyond the village.
But there are conventions to be obeyed, and with the onset
of war Ella finds she cannot delay much longer.

Against this background, Ella sifts through the vagaries of
her physical and emotional needs and weighs up the value
of two different kinds of love. The circumstances in which
Ella makes her final choice provide a poignant and
fulfilling conclusion to Stan Barstow's perfectly crafted
novel, which is sure to win him new readers.

'A simple tale, told with great clarity and never a wrong
note struck'
HILARY BAILEY, THE GUARDIAN

(GIVE US THIS DAY, the moving sequel to JUST YOU WAIT
AND SEE is also available from Black Swan)

0 552 99341 7

BLACK SWAN

A Kind of Loving
Stan Barstow

As probably the best example of work produced by British
novelists in the 1960s, A KIND OF LOVING is now
regarded as a classic of post-war literature.

Immortalised first as a film and then as a highly-acclaimed
television series, Stan Barstow's novel is as alive and as
relevant today as when its author was described on first
publication as having 'warmth, liveliness, honesty and
compassion'
SUNDAY TIMES

The first of a trilogy (THE WATCHERS ON THE SHORE
and THE RIGHT TRUE END are both published in Black
Swan), A KIND OF LOVING tells how young Vic Brown
comes to terms – the hard way – with adult life and his
feelings for the beautiful but demanding Ingrid.

0 552 99186 4

BLACK SWAN

TITLES BY STAN BARSTOW
AVAILABLE FROM BLACK SWAN

THE PRICES SHOWN BELOW WERE CORRECT AT THE TIME OF GOING TO PRESS. HOW-
EVER TRANSWORLD PUBLISHERS RESERVE THE RIGHT TO SHOW NEW RETAIL PRICES
ON COVERS WHICH MAY DIFFER FROM THOSE PREVIOUSLY ADVERTISED IN THE TEXT
OR ELSEWHERE.

☐	99186 4	**A KIND OF LOVING**	£4.99
☐	99189 9	**THE WATCHERS ON THE SHORE**	£4.99
☐	99187 2	**THE RIGHT TRUE END**	£4.99
☐	99184 8	**ASK ME TOMORROW**	£4.99
☐	99390 5	**A BROTHER'S TALE**	£4.99
☐	99159 7	**THE GLAD EYE AND OTHER STORIES**	£3.50
☐	99341 7	**JUST YOU WAIT AND SEE**	£3.95
☐	99434 0	**GIVE US THIS DAY**	£4.99
☐	99193 7	**A RAGING CALM**	£4.95
☐	99176 7	**JOBY**	£3.50

*All Black Swan Books are available at your bookshop or newsagent, or can be ordered from
the following address:*

Corgi/Bantam Books,
Cash Sales Department,
P.O. Box 11, Falmouth, Cornwall TR10 9EN

Please send a cheque or postal order (no currency) and allow 80p for postage and packing for
the first book plus 20p for each additional book ordered up to a maximum charge of £2.00 in UK.

B.F.P.O. customers please allow 80p for the first book and 20p for each additional book.

Overseas customers, including Eire, please allow £1.50 for postage and packing for the first
book, £1.00 for the second book, and 30p for each subsequent title ordered.

NAME (Block Letters) ....

ADDRESS ....

....